A secret memory...

What happened next that spring afternoon is something I know Jeddy remembers. I can see us standing there, two raw-boned boys beside the bootleg crate, seagulls wheeling overhead, making dives on a tidal pool up the beach from us. Almost as an afterthought we wandered toward this pool, not expecting to see anything. It came into view with no more drama than if it had been a sodden piece of driftwood lying on the sand: a naked human leg.

Patricia Lee Gauch, editor

PUFFIN BOOKS
Published by the Penguin Group
Penguin Young Readers Group, 345 Hudson Street, New York, New York 10014, U.S.A.
Penguin Group (Canada), 90 Eglinton Avenue East, Suite 700, Toronto, Ontario, Canada M4P 2Y3
(a division of Pearson Penguin Canada Inc.)
Penguin Books Ltd, 80 Strand, London WC2R 0RL, England
Penguin Ireland, 25 St Stephen's Green, Dublin 2, Ireland (a division of Penguin Books Ltd)
Penguin Group (Australia), 250 Camberwell Road, Camberwell, Victoria 3124, Australia
(a division of Pearson Australia Group Pty Ltd)
Penguin Books India Pvt Ltd, 11 Community Centre, Panchsheel Park, New Delhi - 110 017, India
Penguin Group (NZ), 67 Apollo Drive, Rosedale, North Shore 0745, Auckland, New Zealand
(a division of Pearson New Zealand Ltd.)
Penguin Books (South Africa) (Pty) Ltd, 24 Sturdee Avenue,
Rosebank, Johannesburg 2196, South Africa

Registered Offices: Penguin Books Ltd, 80 Strand, London WC2R 0RL, England

First published in the United States of America by Philomel Books,
a division of Penguin Young Readers Group, 2006
This Sleuth edition first published by Puffin Books, a division of Penguin Young Readers Group, 2007

20 19 18 17 16

THE LIBRARY OF CONGRESS HAS CATALOGED THE PHILOMEL BOOKS EDITION AS FOLLOWS:
Lisle, Janet Taylor. Black Duck/ Janet Taylor Lisle.
p. cm.
Summary: Years afterwards, Ruben Hart tells the story of how, in 1929 Newport, Rhode Island,
his family and his best friend's family were caught up in the violent competition among
groups trying to control the local rum-smuggling trade.
ISBN: 0-399-23963-4 (hc)
[1. Prohibition—Fiction. 2. Friendship—Fiction. 3. Adventure and adventurers—Fiction.
4. Gangsters—Fiction. 5. Newport (R.I.)—History—20th century—Fiction.]
I. Title
PZ7.L6912Bla 2006
[Fic]—dc22   2005023845

Puffin Sleuth ISBN: 978-0-14-240902-2

Printed in the United States of America
Design by Semadar Megged.

BLACK DUCK

JANET TAYLOR LISLE

For Richard Lisle, with love.

Newport Daily Journal, December 30, 1929

COAST GUARDS KILL THREE SUSPECTED RUM RUNNERS

FIRE ON UNARMED SPEEDBOAT BLACK DUCK WITH LARGE CARGO OF LIQUOR

NEWPORT, DEC. 30—Three alleged rum runners were killed by machine gun fire and another man was wounded near Newport shortly before 3 o'clock Sunday morning, according to the Coast Guard. The men were in a 50-foot speedboat well-known locally as the Black Duck.

The boat, carrying a cargo of 300 cases of smuggled liquor, was stumbled on in dense fog by Coast Guard Patrol Boat 290. A burst of machine gun fire killed all three men instantly in the pilot house. A fourth crew member was shot through the hand. No arms were found on board.

"The shooting is unfortunate but clearly justified by U.S. Prohibition law forbidding the trade or consumption of liquor anywhere in the United States," a Coast Guard spokesman said in a statement to reporters last night. "These rogue smugglers threaten our communities and must be stopped."

Other details were not available as authorities kept them guarded.

The Interview

A RUMRUNNER HAD LIVED IN TOWN, ONE OF the notorious outlaws who smuggled liquor during the days of Prohibition, that was the rumor. David Peterson heard he might still be around.

Where?

No one knew exactly. It was all so long ago.

Well, who was he?

This was equally vague. Someone said to ask at the general store across from the church.

It would be a miracle if the man was still alive, David thought. He'd be over eighty. If he were anywhere, he'd probably be in a nursing home by now.

But it turned out he wasn't. He still lived in town. Ruben Hart was his name.

The number listed in the telephone book doesn't answer. There is an address, though. David has his mother drop him off at the end of the driveway. It's June. School is over. He tells her not to wait.

The house is gray shingle, hidden behind a mass of bushes that have grown up in front of the windows. David isn't surprised. It's what happens with old people's homes. Plantings meant to be low hedges or decorative bushes sprout up. Over time, if no one pays attention, they get out of control. David's family is in the landscaping business and he knows about the power of vegetation. He's seen whole trees growing through the floor of a porch, and climbing vines with their fingers in the attic. Left to its own devices, nature runs amok.

David knocks on the front door. After a long pause, an old fellow in a baggy gray sweater opens up. David tells him straight out why he's come: he's looking for a story to get in the local paper.

They won't hire me, but the editor says if I come up with a good story, he'll print it. I want to be a reporter, he announces, all in one breath.

Is that so? the man says. His face has the rumpled look of a well-used paper bag, all lines and creases. But his eyes are shrewd.

I'm a senior in high school, David explains to build up his case. It's a slight exaggeration. He'll be a freshman next fall.

He receives a skeptical stare.

Then the man, who is in fact Ruben Hart himself, *still kicking,* as he says with a sly glint of his glasses, invites David in.

My wife's in the kitchen. We can go in the parlor.

David has never before heard anyone say that word, *parlor,* to describe a room in a house. He's read it in stories from English class, though, and knows what one is.

The chairs are formal and hard as a rock, just as you'd expect.

I suppose you're here to find out about the old days, Mr. Hart says. His voice is raspy-sounding, as if he doesn't use it much.

I am.

Must be the liquor Prohibition back in the 1920s you're interested in, rumrunners and hijackers, fast boats and dark nights.

Yes, sir!

I wasn't in it.

You weren't? David frowns. *I heard you were.*

I wasn't.

Well.

I guess that's that, Mr. Hart says. *Sorry to disappoint you.*

Did you know anyone who was? David asks.

I might've. Mr. Hart's glasses glint again.

Could you talk about them?

No.

That was the end of their first meeting.

A week later, David tries again. He's done some research this time, found a newspaper article from 1929 about the Coast Guard gunning down some unarmed rumrunners, and learned the names of beaches around there where the liquor was brought in.

The first rumrunners were local fishermen who wanted to make an extra buck for their families. They'd sneak cases of booze onshore off boats that brought the stuff down from Canada or up from the Bahamas. But there was too much money to be made, as there is in the drug trade today. Hardened criminals came in and formed gangs. People were shot up and murdered. The business turned vicious.

My wife's gone out, we can sit in the kitchen, Mr. Hart says this time.

When they settle, David has his plan of attack ready.

I don't want to bother you, but I read about some things and wondered if I could check them out with you. Nothing personal, just some facts.

Such as? The old man's eyes are wary.

Was Brown's Beach a drop for liquor? I read it was.

I guess there's no harm in agreeing to that. Everybody in town knew it.

And were there hidden storage cellars under the floor of the old barn out behind Riley's General Store? Across from the church, you know where I mean?

They're still there, as far as I know.

One other thing, David says. *There was a famous rum-running boat around here named the* Black Duck . . .

That was the end of their second meeting.

The man closes up, won't even make eye contact. He says his heart's acting funny and he's got to take a pill. Five minutes later David is heading back out the driveway. He hitches home this time rather than wait for his mother. He's touched on something, he knows it. There's a story there. How to pry it out of the old geezer?

He's still wondering a week later when, surprise of all

surprises, Mr. Hart calls him. He's managed to ferret out David's home number from among the dozens of Petersons in the telephone book.

I'll talk to you a bit. An old friend of mine is ill. You've been on my mind.

David can't see the connection between himself and some old friend, but he gets a ride over there as soon as he can. His father drives him this time, grumbling, *You're making me late. What's wrong with riding a bicycle? In my day, we went everywhere under our own steam.*

David doesn't answer. In a year and a half he'll be old enough to drive himself and won't need to put up with irritating comments like this.

Sorry about your friend being sick, he says to Mr. Hart. They're in the kitchen again. The wife has gone away to visit her brother out of state.

Took a turn for the worse the beginning of the week, Mr Hart says. *Jeddy McKenzie. He and I grew up together here. His dad used to be police chief in this town.*

He gazes speculatively at David. *Ever hear of Chief Ralph McKenzie?*

David says no.

Well, that was way back, during these Prohibition days you're so interested in. The law against liquor got passed and the government dumped it on the local cops to enforce. That was a laugh. What'd they think would happen? Afterward, Jeddy moved away, to North Carolina. I always hoped I'd see him again. We were close at one time. Had adventures.

What adventures? David asks.

Mr. Hart's eyes flick over him, as if he still has grave doubts about this interview. He goes ahead anyway.

Ever seen a dead body?

David shakes his head.

We found one washed up down on Coulter's Beach.

David knows where Coulter's Beach is. He swims off there sometimes. *Was it a rumrunner?* he asks.

Mr. Hart doesn't answer. He has watery blue eyes that wink around behind his glasses' thick lenses. It's hard to get a handle on his expression.

This was in the spring, 1929. Smuggling was in high gear. Thousands of cases of liquor coming in every month up and down this coast. Outside racketeers creeping in like worms to a carcass, smelling the money. People look back now and think those days were romantic, all high jinks and derring-do. They're mistaken.

David has brought a notepad along, expecting to jot down interesting facts. *Not romantic,* he writes at the top of the page. (What are *high jinks*?) After that, he forgets to write. Mr. Hart's raspy voice takes over the room.

So, Jeddy McKenzie and I came on this body.

ON COULTER'S BEACH

THE WIND HAD BLOWN IT IN.

A stiff sou'wester was in charge that day, shoving the waves against the shore like a big impatient hand. Jeddy's head never could keep a cap on in a blow. I remember how he walked bent over, holding his brim down with both hands. I stalked beside him, eyes on the sand.

"Clean beach," I'd say gloomily whenever we rounded a corner.

We'd been hunting for lobster pots since lunch and would have gone on till dinner if not for the interruption. Marked pots returned to their owners paid ten cents apiece. We were fourteen years old and in dire need of funds. You couldn't get a red penny out of your parents in those days. They didn't have anything to spare.

"There's got to be some! It blew like stink all night," Jeddy shouted over the wind.

"Well, it's blowing like murder right now," I cried back, without an inkling of how true this was about to become.

We rounded a spuming sand dune to a burst of noise. Down the beach, braying seagulls circled at the water's edge.

"Something's driving bait. Maybe a shark," Jeddy said. "Those gulls are getting in on the kill."

I shaded my eyes. "No, it's something else. I can see something floating in the water."

"Dead shark, then."

"Or a dead seal. Too small for a shark. Come on."

We took off at a jog, wind tearing at our clothes. When we got there, though, all we saw was a busted-up wooden crate knocking around in the waves. Nothing was inside, but we recognized its type. It was a bootleg case, a thing we'd come across before on the beach. If you were lucky, and we never were that I can recall, there'd be bottles still wedged inside—whiskey, vodka, brandy, even champagne—smuggled liquor that could bring a good price if you knew what to do with it. Jeddy and I weren't lawbreakers. We'd never even had a drink. But like a lot of folks along that coast we weren't against keeping our eyes open if there was a chance of profit in it.

"Coast Guard must have been sniffing around here last night," Jeddy said. "Looks like somebody had to dump their cargo fast."

"Maybe. Could be it's left over from a landing. They've been bringing stuff into the dock down at Tyler's Lane."

"How d'you know that?"

"Saw them," I boasted, then wished I hadn't. It was no secret that Jeddy's dad was on the lookout for rumrunners. Police Chief Ralph McKenzie was a stickler for the law.

Jeddy gave me a look. "You saw somebody landing their goods? At night?"

I shut my trap and inspected a schooner passing out to sea. I knew something Jeddy didn't.

"What were you doing at Tyler's at night?" he demanded. "It's way across town from your house. Ruben Hart! You're fibbing, right?"

"Well." I gave the crate a kick.

"I thought so! Next you're going to say it was the *Black Duck*."

"Maybe it was!"

"You're a liar, that's for sure. Nobody ever sees the *Duck*. My dad's been chasing her for years and never even come close. She's got twin airplane engines, you know. She does over thirty knots."

I glared at him. "I know."

"So did you see her or not?"

"Maybe I heard somebody talking."

"When?"

"Couple of days ago. It's dark of the moon this week. That's when they bring the stuff in."

"Who was talking?"

"I better not say. You'd have to tell your dad."

"I wouldn't. Honest."

I shrugged and gazed across the water to where the lighthouse was standing up on its rock, high and white as truth itself.

"Come on. I'd only have to tell him if he asked me direct, and why would he do that?" Jeddy said. "Did some-body see the *Black Duck* come in at Tyler's dock?"

"Listen, I don't know," I said, backing off. "I heard a rumor there was a landing, that's all. Whoever did it could've cracked some cases to pay off the shore crew that helped unload. That's one way they pay them. Everybody gets a few bottles."

"Well, you should know," Jeddy said, sulkily. "Your dad is probably in deep with the whole thing."

"He is not!" I drew up my defenses at this. "My dad would never break the law. He might not agree with it, but he wouldn't break it."

My father was Carl Hart, manager of Riley's General Store in town. He was a big man with a big personality, known for speaking his mind in a moment of heat, but there was nothing underhanded in him. He dealt fair and square no matter who you were, and often he was more than fair. Quietly, without even Mr. Riley knowing, he'd help out folks going through hard times by carrying their overdue accounts till they could pay. He wouldn't take any thanks for it, either, which is why my mother would find a couple of fresh-caught bluefish on our front porch some mornings, or a slab of smoked ham or an apple pie.

"Now, Carl, what is it you've done to deserve this?" she'd ask, raising an eyebrow.

He'd shake his head like it was nothing, and never answer.

My father was tough on me growing up. He was an old-fashioned believer in discipline and hard work, far beyond what was fair or necessary, it seemed to me. There never was much warmth or fun between us, the way some boys have with their dads, but one thing I was sure of: he was an honest man. Whatever mischief was going on along our shores at night—and you'd have had to be both blind and deaf back then not to know there was a lot—it wouldn't have anything to do with him.

Jeddy knew it, too. "Your dad wouldn't break any law," he admitted. "I was only saying that."

"I knew you didn't mean it," I said.

We almost never fought. Whatever Jeddy thought or felt, I understood and respected, and I'd step back and make allowances for it. He watched out for me the same way. I guess you could say we'd sort of woven together.

Our mothers had grown up in town and been friends themselves all the way through school. When they married our dads, they became friends, too. In the early days there was a steady stream of lendings and borrowings, emergency soups and neighborly stews between our houses, the sort of thing that goes on so easily in a small town. Then, in the middle of one winter, Jeddy's mother got sick. It turned out to be the flu that took so many that year.

Her death stunned everyone in town, but it struck the McKenzies like an iron fist. Eileen was her name, and she'd been the heart of the family, the strong one in the house. Jeddy's dad just collapsed. For a while, he didn't go anywhere or do anything.

Jeddy was seven at the time, in the first grade with

me. I remember how I'd walk over in the afternoons after school and sit on his front porch in case he wanted to come down and play. Sometimes he did and sometimes he didn't. I'd stay awhile—the place was too quiet to even think of knocking—then go off if he didn't appear. We both knew without saying it that I'd be back the next day. It was a way we'd worked out to help him get through.

Jeddy's dad had been head man on a local chicken farm, but soon he quit that and began to commute over to Portsmouth to train for police work. The state force was just starting up. It pulled him away from old connections, including my parents, and maybe that's what he wanted. Even when he was hired a year later for the job of our police chief, he kept his distance from us. He never spoke to anyone about the blow he'd suffered, but thinking back, I wonder if he wasn't still trying to depend on his wife for a strength he didn't have. Anyone visiting at the McKenzies' could've seen it. He was keeping her around, strange as that sounds.

Her coat and hat hung on a hook in the hall, as if she'd only stepped out for a moment. Her wedding china was on display in the parlor cabinet. Her sheet music sat on the piano. Her bold handwriting filled the book of recipes that lay open, more often than not, on the counter in the kitchen where Marina, Jeddy's older sister, was now in charge. She'd been a frightened nine-year-old when her mother had died. Seven years later, at sixteen, she was running the house.

It was Marina who served us supper when Jeddy asked

me to stay over evenings. It was she who washed up after, darned her father's socks, hung the laundry and took it down. She changed the beds, swept the floors, hauled in coal for the stove. With the sleeves of her school blouse rolled tight above her elbows (at this time, she was still only a high school sophomore) and one of her mother's cotton aprons wrapped double around her waist, Marina handled all the jobs a grown woman would. I couldn't get used to that, seeing a girl that age taking on what she did. Only a certain watchful gaze she leveled at the world gave a glimpse into what it must have cost her.

"I'd tell you if I knew who it was at Tyler's, really I would," I said to Jeddy that day on the beach, to make things right between us.

He nodded. "I know you would. And I wouldn't tell my dad."

"Of course not."

"It'd be just between us."

"Always has been, always will be," I announced. I couldn't meet his eyes though. I'd already broken that trust. There was something I wasn't telling him, something I couldn't.

Maybe he suspected, because he gave me a long stare. Then he let it go, didn't say any more about it. I wonder, though, when he thinks back—as I know he has done plenty of times over the years, just like me—does he remember that conversation the way I do, as the first crack in our friendship? I wish I could ask him.

What happened next that spring afternoon is something I know Jeddy remembers. I can see us standing there, two raw-boned boys beside the bootleg crate, seagulls wheeling overhead, making dives on a tidal pool up the beach from us. Almost as an afterthought we wandered toward this pool, not expecting to see anything. It came into view with no more drama than if it had been a sodden piece of driftwood lying on the sand: a naked human leg.

A DARK-RIMMED HOLE

IT'S ODD HOW A SHOCKING SIGHT CAN SHAKE your mind so you don't at first register the whole, just the small, almost comical details. Like the hand complete with fancy gold wristwatch, wedding band and neatly clipped fingernails we saw bobbing on the water's surface as we came toward the pool. Above it, swathed in a shawl of brown seaweed, a rubbery-looking shoulder peeked out, white as a girl's. Above that, a bloated face the color of slate; two sightless eyes, open. And there in his neck, what was that? I saw a small dark-rimmed hole.

The body was surrounded by floating shreds of what had once been a fancy evening suit. The feet were bare, with the same wrinkly soles anyone would get who stayed in a bathtub too long.

"Looks like he's been in the water awhile," Jeddy said. "Is it somebody?"

He meant, "Is it somebody we know."

"Don't think so," I said. "Anyhow, he was shot."

"Where?"

"In the neck. See there?"

Jeddy leaned forward to look. The hole was in the skin

just above the collarbone. "Oh," he said, and stepped back fast.

"We could check his pockets," he suggested. "See if he's got a wallet or something with his name on it."

"Go ahead," I said. "I'll hold your hat."

He took it off and gave it to me, then bent to touch the body, which rocked a bit under his hand.

"Maybe we shouldn't disturb anything."

"Maybe not," I said, as squeamish as he was.

"My dad would look if he were here."

"He'd have to."

Jeddy squared himself and went forward again. Reaching into the water, he felt the sodden sides of what remained of the dead man's pants for where the pockets would be.

"I can't feel anything."

"Try his jacket."

Jed patted down the black floating garment and shook his head. "Guess he lost everything at sea."

"Or he was frisked after they shot him," I said. "Anything in his back pockets?"

"You do it," Jeddy said. He'd had enough.

I went forward and felt around, trying not to brush up against the corpse's skin. It had a cold, blubbery feel that turned my stomach. My hands ran into something. I brought out a pipe and a sodden satchel of tobacco.

"Guess he was a smoker."

Jeddy took them for a look, then handed them back. "Are you sure that's all?"

"Yes."

"We need to tell someone."

"Your dad."

"Let's go back to my house. I can call him from there."

After this, though, action seemed beyond us. For a time we stood rooted in place, staring at the dead man, and at the pool of gray water he lay in, and at the gulls who floated on the incoming swells just offshore, watching our movements with cold yellow eyes. Death was no more to them than a ready-made meal. Neither of us had seen a drowned man before, not to mention a corpse with a bullet hole in its neck.

"I bet he was with the mob," said Jeddy, who had no clearer idea than I did at this time what that might be. "Maybe he was in on the landings at Tyler's Lane."

"Wearing an evening suit?"

"Well, maybe he's a high roller from Newport and he tried to double-cross somebody and they found out."

"Or maybe they double-crossed him."

The newspapers were full of such stories. My mother tried to keep me from reading them, but I got around her on that as I did on most things. Al Capone and his Chicago gangsters were in the headlines daily. In New York City, Lucky Luciano was fighting it out with a couple of other gangs, and from all accounts blood flowed regularly in the streets. It was thugs gunning down thugs for the most part, battling over territorial rights to extortion and pay-offs.

Right up in Providence there was Danny Walsh, one of

the big-time bootleggers. He was always having people bumped off. You could tip your hat the wrong way at Danny Walsh and that was it, your number was up. To Jeddy and me, all this underworld activity seemed glamorous. We knew the cast of characters, we knew the lingo. Like a lot of kids at that time, we followed gangland murders the same way we read the comics.

This body was real.

"Whoever he is, those gulls are going after him soon as we leave," Jeddy said.

I examined the waiting flock. "You think they'd eat him?"

"Sure, why not. Gulls eat everything."

"Well, there's nothing to cover him with."

"Scare 'em off," Jeddy ordered.

For the next quarter hour, we threw stones and yelled and ran out in the water to make them fly away, which was a waste of time. Not a gull batted an eye. The whole group simply paddled sedately out of reach, then turned to stare at us again. Jeddy flung his cap on the ground. His temper could flare up quicker than mine.

"Stupid birds!"

"The only thing is to get somebody back here fast as we can."

"All right. Let's go."

We began to run down the beach, stopping to heave more threatening volleys at the gulls. Even before we reached the first bend, we could see the flock edging closer to shore, getting ready to pounce.

"Cannibals," Jeddy panted. "Wish I had a gun."

Around the end of Coulter's Point, we let loose and raced for our bikes.

The person who answered at the police station was the force's part-time bookkeeper, Mildred Cumming. She sounded sleepy when she took Jeddy's call, but she'd snapped to a moment later.

"A dead man? . . . Shot! Anybody from around here? . . . Right. I'm getting Charlie. Hold on, kiddo, don't you go anywhere."

From the stairs in Jeddy's front hall, I heard everything. The McKenzies' telephone was new to the house, a wall model tucked into a special alcove under the staircase. The town had paid to have it installed so Chief McKenzie could take calls at home. Jeddy wasn't supposed to use it, but this was an emergency.

There was a long wait while Mildred went to get Charlie Pope, deputy sergeant at the station, who was most likely across the street at Weedie's Coffee Shop, jawing and reading the papers. Normally, there wasn't much that went on day to day in a hamlet our size. People knew each other too well. With only one road into town, any suspicious character who didn't get noticed on the way in was sure to be pulled over on the way out. The whole police force amounted to only two individuals, neither of whom cared to carry a gun.

"This is me. Yeah, I heard," Charlie told Jeddy when he got came on. "It's a man, you say?"

Jeddy said it was.

"What's he wearing, could you see?"

Jeddy explained about the evening suit.

"Your dad's not here. Gone to New Bedford to see a fellow. Back in a couple of hours. I'll try to get a message to him. You boys stay where y'are. I'll be at your place soon as I can."

"We'll meet you at the beach," Jeddy said. "There's a pack of gulls down there getting at the body. We'll stand guard till you come."

This caused an explosion on the other end of the line.

"You stay put!" Charlie's voice boomed out, so loud that Jeddy jerked the receiver away from his ear. "I don't want you going down on that beach again! Now that's an order!"

Jeddy rolled his eyes and said all right. About then, the front door opposite me opened and Marina came in, her dark hair loose and streaming from the wind. A single glance at Jeddy on the phone was all she needed.

"What happened?" she asked me.

"We found a body washed up on the beach."

"A fisherman?"

"Probably not."

"What beach?"

"Coulter's."

"What were you doing down there?"

"Looking for lobster pots."

I avoided her direct gaze. With her hair blown that way and her face glowing from the cold walk home,

Marina McKenzie was almost unbearably pretty. I was at the age where it embarrassed me to find myself noticing this.

"Did you get any?" she asked.

"No," I said to the floor.

Jeddy finished his conversation with Charlie and put the telephone receiver cautiously back on its hook.

"We're to wait," he informed me. To his sister he said, "Charlie Pope's coming."

Marina wrinkled her nose. "That weasel, why him?"

"Dad's in New Bedford. They're calling him."

"Is it anybody from around here?"

"We don't think so. He's all dressed up and has a gold wristwatch. A bunch of seagulls were on him. We shooed them off."

"Maybe he fell off the New York boat," Marina said.

"He was shot," Jeddy said. He followed his sister down the hall and into the kitchen. "There's a bullet hole in his neck."

Behind on the stairs, I waited for what Marina would have to say about this, but nothing came. That was like her. She was a careful person who tended to keep her thoughts to herself. Not that she was shy. She knew how to speak up when she wanted, even to her own father, the chief of police. She just wasn't a gabber like some girls her age. It was another thing I'd noticed about her.

I heard the sound of a cupboard door opening and closing. She was starting supper, as she did every afternoon at about this time. I knew that house, felt easy there, more comfortable than in my own. At home my father loomed large in my sight, and whatever was talked about, whatever was thought, seemed to revolve around him. Often it had to do with the store, where I worked most afternoons, though never hard enough to please him. He'd set a standard of performance that was beyond me, or so it seemed to me then, and though he never expressed it, I was aware of an undercurrent of disappointment in his dealings with me. It was as if he knew me better than I knew myself, and had detected some weakness at my center. Against this flaw, whatever it was, I was in a constant state of struggle.

At the McKenzies', the pressure lifted. The family was just this side of poor. Chief McKenzie drew a good deal less salary than what my father made managing the store, and there were few luxuries. The only bathroom was downstairs off the kitchen. There was no hot water. Upstairs, the rooms were still without electricity—Jeddy and I went to bed by candlelight when I stayed over. Everywhere the furnishings were cheap and old.

None of this mattered to me. I'd come to love the dim light and dusty corners, the worn armchairs and drab curtains. Nothing was ever moved or changed. Marina had barely enough time to keep up with daily tasks, and none at all for the mail-order frills and home improvements my mother was so fond of. Then again, even if there had been time, and money, change was not something those who lived in that house would have wanted.

On the wall opposite the stairs where I sat that afternoon was an old photograph of Jeddy's mother. It was a formal studio portrait that had been painted with a wash of color to give her face a more lifelike appearance. Mrs. McKenzie had had dark hair and serious eyes like Marina. She held her head the same upright way her daughter did, and a wrinkle on her forehead was identical to one that rose on Marina's forehead in thoughtful moments.

I'd come across Chief McKenzie staring at this portrait of his wife more than a few times, and I could guess why. She had a gaze that gave you strength. That day on the stairs, I remember how Eileen McKenzie's eyes seemed suddenly to lock onto mine, as if she'd recognized me and was asking me to stay; as if she'd accepted me as a member of her family. I knew it was silly, but I smiled and nodded back.

"I'm frying chicken for supper," Marina's voice said from the kitchen.

"Can we have potato salad?" Jeddy's voice asked.

"If you peel," Marina replied severely.

"Can Ruben stay? It's Saturday."

"If he wants. Tell him he can use the telephone to call his mother. But he has to peel, too."

"Ruben!" Jeddy called. "Want to stay for supper? Marina's frying chicken."

I got up and went in the kitchen.

"What are you grinning about?" Marina asked me, her mother's stern eyes on my face.

"I don't know, nothing."

"You've just found a body on the beach and now you're grinning like a hyena and you don't know why?"

"Nope," I said, grinning wider than ever.

Something about the dopey way I said this must have struck her funny, because she turned her head to hide a smile.

"Ruben Hart, have you no respect for the dead?" she said, trying for a prudish tone. It was no use; she started to laugh.

"Marina!" Jeddy exclaimed.

"I'm sorry!" she cried, and put a hand over her mouth. "I don't know why it's so funny. It's Ruben's fault for getting me going."

She sent me an accusing look and turned back to the chicken. But a second later she began to laugh again. Soon, she was shaking with laughter.

Jeddy and I eyed each other in alarm. We'd never seen her like this. Jeddy scowled, and I would have, too, except that suddenly I found this breakdown to be wonderful beyond words. All the strictness had gone out of Marina's face, which collapsed and turned pink no matter how she tried to stop it.

"Don't look at me!" she gasped, wiping her eyes. "A person has the right to laugh in her own kitchen!"

Jeddy and I stood before her, solemn as two owls, though there must've been the twitch of a grin on my face.

I never did find out what set Marina off that day, but

it changed the way I thought about her. She was still far ahead of me, an older girl who could make me blush just by meeting my eyes. But I'd caught sight of another person living inside, someone wilder and freer, less bound by the rules around her than she allowed others to see. That was something back then to recognize in a girl, and it filled me with excitement. I couldn't have begun to explain why.

THE DISAPPEARANCE

SUPPER WAS LAID OUT, READY TO BE COOKED, when Charlie Pope finally arrived at the house three hours later. By then, it was after six. Jeddy and I were in a fume.

"He'll be eaten up!"

"What took you so long?"

"Hold your horses, we'll get there soon enough. Mildred got through to your dad," Charlie said to Jeddy. "He's on his way."

Marina threw on a coat and followed us out the door.

"Well, if it isn't the Queen of Sheba. Out for a bit of fun?" I heard Charlie say to her in a sarcastic voice.

"I'll come if I want."

"Course you will, honey. You always do what you want, don't you?"

Marina brushed past him and we went out to Charlie's car for the drive to the beach. I saw how careful she was to keep her distance from him. She sat in the backseat with me, arms folded across her chest. Something was wrong between Charlie and Marina. Jeddy didn't notice, but I did.

The sun was low in the west when we arrived at the

beach. The strong winds of that afternoon were dying. The air smelled of seaweed. We walked single file down the sandy path toward the shore. Jeddy, in the lead, slowed and lifted his head.

"What's that noise?"

We all cocked an ear. Through the crash and roll of waves came a high, droning buzz. It grew louder as we marched over a rise in the dunes. Jeddy pointed across the bay.

"It's an airplane!"

I looked and saw a tiny gray form floating above the Newport peninsula. Airplanes weren't an everyday sight at that time. We all stopped to watch.

"Probably some tycoon coming in from New York," Charlie said. "I read in the papers how they've built a landing field over there. Come and go like thieves in the night."

He walked ahead, suddenly impatient. "Let's get moving. I haven't got all day."

We set off again, and it wasn't long before Jeddy and I were squinting along the beach, expecting to see the pack of gulls hard at work at the water's edge. The closer we got, the more we couldn't see one bird.

"That's strange," I said. "Gulls never give up."

When we came up on the place, the reason was clear. The shallow pool where the body had lain was empty.

Jeddy stared in disbelief. "It was here!"

"It was," I agreed.

Charlie glanced up the beach, then out to sea. The

dead man could not have floated away. The tide was too low, still going out, in fact.

"The flock of gulls was there," Jeddy said, pointing. "They were coming after him when we left."

"Must've been hungry," Charlie said, flashing a grin at Marina. She turned her head away. To Jeddy, he said, "You're sure this was the place?"

"Yes, sir. It was here!"

"Lying just where, would you say?"

"In this little pool of water. Half in, half out."

"A man, you said, and he was all dressed up?"

Jeddy explained again about the torn evening suit, the watch, the wedding band and the seaweed.

"He had bare feet," I added. "His face was kind of mushed in."

"Well, there's no sign of him now. No sign of anything," Charlie said, sounding oddly satisfied. "If somebody came and dragged him off, there'd be marks, wouldn't you think? There's not even any footprints."

We all looked. The beach was smooth, except for the tracks we'd just made coming across the sand. Woven in among them were our first tracks, Jeddy's and mine. No one else had been on that stretch of shore for the last eight hours.

"They might have come in by sea," I ventured.

Charlie shook his head. "In here? Naw. It's too shallow for a boat."

That was true. The shelf of the beach extended way out into the water.

"Well, listen. There's something else," Jeddy said. He sounded desperate. "There was an empty wooden case that was washed in with the body. A bootlegger's case. That's gone, too."

Charlie's expression changed at this.

"You think this guy was a rumrunner?"

"I don't know. I'm just saying . . ."

"How could you tell he was shot?" Charlie wanted to know.

"We saw a hole in his neck, at the bottom," Jeddy said.

"Yeah, but was there any blood?"

Jed shook his head. "It must've all washed away."

"Any sign of bruising?"

"I didn't see any."

"This hole was from a bullet, you say?"

"Yes, sir."

"And how did you make that out?"

"Well, I don't know. It just seemed that it was."

"There's a lot of things that 'seem,' " Charlie said, glancing over at Marina again.

"I know, but this body—"

"Especially with things like bodies," Charlie snapped at Jeddy. "There's a lot you can't tell from just looking at them. I mean, there are officers whose job it is to say what happened and how it was done and when and where and so forth." He stopped and gave Jeddy and me a look.

"The thing is, I wouldn't be spreading the rumor of somebody that's shot washing up here," he said. "Since we don't even know for sure that he was shot."

Jeddy said, "Oh."

"In fact, if you can keep the news down about this body at all, it would be best."

"It would?"

"And you, too, Marina. Keep it under your bonnet."

"My *what*?" she lashed out. "And who says? You?"

"Your *dad* and me," Charlie answered. "We're going to be reporting this supposed body to the proper authorities, and they're going to be reporting to those above them, and it won't do any good to have rumors flying about."

"Supposed body!" Jeddy exclaimed. "What does that mean?"

"It means just what it means."

"There wasn't anything 'supposed' about this body!" Jeddy said. I saw he was losing his temper. There wasn't much good that could come from that.

"When you find out, will you let us know who it was?" I asked Charlie.

"I might," he answered. "And then again, we may never know exactly."

"Exactly what?"

"What happened."

Marina laughed out loud. "I can see this investigation is off to a good start," she said.

Charlie glanced at her angrily, turned his back and walked off.

"So, is that it?" I called after him.

"It is," he spat over his shoulder. "Whew! Seaweed stinks to high heaven around here."

There was nothing more to be done. Charlie was determined to drop the case. Even Jeddy's father, who came a few minutes later, gave us a stern look, as if he was displeased that such a thing as a body should have turned up and been found by anyone, let alone his own son. Now that it had conveniently disappeared, he seemed in no mood to discuss it further.

"I stopped by the house and saw that supper's ready to be cooked," he said to Marina. "Shouldn't you be back there getting to it?"

She spun on her heel without answering and strode away. Charlie and Chief McKenzie went off down the beach for a private chat while Jeddy and I waited. Ten minutes later, the four of us set out after her for home.

Jeddy swung into step with his father. Whatever happened, Jeddy never stayed mad at his dad for long. You could see how he revered the man by the way he walked beside him, matching his stride.

"Hey, Dad, Ruben is coming, too," he said. "Marina said it was all right."

"Coming to what?" Chief McKenzie glanced down at him.

"Supper," Jeddy said. "He called his mother. It's all set."

"Well, he can't. Not tonight, whatever Marina said."

"But why?"

The chief shook his head. "Because I say so."

"But Marina invited him! And it's Saturday night."

Chief McKenzie glared. "I don't care what night it is,

I've had enough fuss and furor for one day!" he thundered. We all looked at him in astonishment.

"What are you staring at?" he shouted. "Marina's not the head of this house, whatever she may think. Take a rain check, Ruben, all right? Tell your folks I'm sorry. We'll see you another time."

"Yes, sir. All right," I said, and that was that. No one spoke another word the whole way down the beach, or in the chief's car going back to the McKenzies'. I picked up my bike and scooted for home like a dog in disgrace.

Marina was already back by that time. She'd taken the walking path across the Point that cut between the roads. I saw the white of her apron through the kitchen window as I pedaled by. At the last minute, she looked out and gave me a wave.

That made me feel better. Marina always was a great one for bucking a person up. She could keep her head in murky weather, too, which was a good thing because, with the arrival of that body, murk is what was heading for us. Jeddy and I couldn't see it yet, but the fog was out there, sifting and swirling, already beginning to close in around the McKenzies' house.

The Interview

THE OLD MAN HAS BEEN TALKING FOR almost an hour when he goes suddenly quiet. (David writes the phrase *swirling fog* down on his notepad, to remind himself where they've left off.)

They sit in silence for a while, Mr. Hart with his eyes closed. Way, way back is where he is, *lost in the folds of time.* David read that somewhere. He didn't really understand what it meant then; now he gets it. Mr. Hart has vanished over the horizon. He's back with his pal Jeddy in 1929. Maybe he knew this was going to happen. Maybe it's why he called up David and decided to talk, as a way of getting there, of revisiting the scene now that Jeddy is so sick. There's some knot in their past that's bothering him.

David has more pressing interests. *So, who was the man on the beach?* he wants to ask. *What's Charlie Pope covering up?* But he can see that the old guy's out of gas. Anyway, it's almost dinnertime and David is due home himself. His mother has a fit if everyone's not there to sit down at 6:30 sharp.

Should I come back tomorrow?

Mr. Hart grunts, eyes still shut.

I'd like to come back tomorrow, David says. *You didn't even get to any smuggling yet, or to the* Black Duck. *I guess you know that the crew on that boat was shot. They wouldn't stop and the Coast Guard opened fire with a machine gun. I read an old newspaper story about it.*

Behind his glasses, Mr. Hart's eyes blink open.

Leave that alone, he rumbles. His eyes close again. David makes his way quietly out of the house, uncertain whether he'll be allowed back.

But the next day when he knocks at a little past noon, Mr. Hart's front door flies open and the old man appears at once.

I've been waiting all morning. Thought you'd chickened out!

David grins. *Sorry, I had to wait for someone to drive me.*

How old did you say you were?

Seventeen?

You seem younger. Mr. Hart fixes him with a spectacled stare.

David avoids his gaze. He wishes he'd never started this bit of fraudulence. It's not like him. He usually keeps things on the level. He was just so afraid he'd be turned away. He wants to get this interview, needs to write this story. He allows the lie to stand.

They sit in the kitchen again, where Mr. Hart takes off his glasses and polishes them energetically on his sweater. His eyes are clearer today, sea-colored. Out from behind their lenses, they have a bright, youthful look. For a second, David catches sight of another Ruben Hart, the boy who was Jeddy's friend, co-explorer of beaches and admirer of older sisters.

Where were we?

Swirling fog, David says. *It's closing in on the McKenzies' house.*

He's brought his notebook again and is determined to make a better attempt at writing things down. His dad is on his case about getting a summer job. He's pressuring David to work in the garden shop that's part of the family landscaping business. So far, David has refused, not an easy stand to take.

Well, don't expect any more handouts from me! his father raged. *It's about time you started supporting your own lifestyle.*

What lifestyle? David had protested. *How can I have a lifestyle when I live at home?*

You know what. Movies, magazines, computer games. All that stuff you buy at the mall. Books.

Books! You mean, for high school next fall? His parents had always paid for those.

They'll cost me a fortune. You could help out if you had a paying job.

I'm trying to get a job with a newspaper, David had explained. *That's what I'm working on. I'm researching a story.*

It hadn't gone over. He had nothing to show for it. His dad is a hands-on guy who measures industry by what he can see: gardens plowed, hedges pruned, lawns seeded. Another reason for the notebook. If David can produce evidence that he's not wasting time, that he has good intentions, his father might cut him some slack. He might realize that David has a plan for his life, even if it doesn't include Peterson's Landscaping and Garden Design.

Who was the dead man in the evening suit, did you ever find out? David asks Mr. Hart now, to get him back on track.

Not right away. There was a clue, though, right under my nose. Something I'd overlooked.

What? David says, ballpoint poised and ready.

MUZZLED

I'D FORGOTTEN THE DEAD MAN'S PIPE.

That night, after supper, I took my jacket upstairs to my room and felt something in the pocket. There was the pipe. I'd stuffed it in without thinking. The leather pouch was there, too, one of the simple foldover packs so many men carried in that day. I turned it around in my hands and opened it. The leaf inside was still damp, alive with scent. An odd feeling swept me that I was out of bounds, prying into something that was not my business. Though that was absurd. The dead man on the beach would never know what I'd taken.

I'd told my father about the body the minute he'd come home from Riley's store that evening. He'd quietly told my mother, and she, in whispers, had informed her sister, my aunt Grace, who lived with us and worked at the post office. Silence seemed to be the way my story was to be treated until Aunt Grace broke ranks, as she often did. She was unmarried, younger than my mother, and known for stating her opinions whatever company she was in. It was not how a woman should conduct herself, my mother believed, and she was always frowning at her and trying to quiet her down.

"So it's come to this, murder on our own shores," Aunt Grace blurted out as the four of us sat eating a late supper that night.

"Who said anything about murder?" asked my father. "A man washed up, that's all we know for sure."

"A man with a bullet hole in his neck, Ruben says. It was just a matter of time," Aunt Grace went on. "And now they've taken to stealing bodies to hide their crimes."

"Come along, Grace. There's no evidence of that," my father said. "It'll be investigated, I'm sure."

"It's the liquor that's causing this! There's no enforcement of our laws."

My mother looked disapproving. "The trouble is that the Coast Guard can't keep up. Our local police have no support. There's too much smuggling going on."

"They could keep up if they wanted," Aunt Grace shot back. "They're in league with it, most of them, making a bundle for themselves under the table."

"Hush, dear," my mother said.

"Well, they are! Just no one wants to say it. What's become of this country? It's all commerce and greed."

"We'll discuss this later, at a more appropriate time," my mother said with arched brows. She meant, "a time when Ruben is not here to listen."

"In case you forgot, I'm the one who found this body!" I protested.

"Ruben, please. We've heard enough about bodies. The subject is now closed," my mother declared with finality.

As if that weren't muzzle enough, my father took me aside after supper to back up Charlie Pope's warning.

"There's no good to be had in stirring up rumors. You and Jed keep a clamp on your mouths and we'll all be the better for it."

"But who would go and take that body? And why didn't Chief McKenzie want to do anything about it?"

"He does want to. And he will, so keep what you saw to yourself. I mean it, Ruben, this is not our affair. Don't go worrying your mother by bringing it up again."

Alone in my room, I closed the pouch with an angry snap and put it down. I picked up the pipe.

It was made of good wood, smooth and glossy, though seawater had mottled it in places. The stem had a fashionable dip with a nice lip. Riley's sold pipes, though none so fine as this one. I ran my finger over the bowl and remembered the expensive wristwatch on the dead man's floating hand. Whoever the man was, he'd had style and the money to support it.

Downstairs, a door slammed. I heard rapid steps leaving the house and looked out in time to see my father getting into the store truck parked in the yard. He often borrowed it for transportation. That evening he was taking it back. There was the whir of the starter, and the distinctive cough of the engine. The headlights came on, bright as twin suns in the dark. The night was moonless again, and perfectly clear. It was just as it had been two nights before, when the only illumination had come from a dusty froth of stars high overhead.

Back at my desk, I stowed the pipe and pouch in a drawer and sat staring out into space. A picture of shadowy forms moving silently up a beach came into my mind.

Tyler's Lane.

I'd been there, of course, despite what I'd let Jeddy think. I hadn't planned to be, never would have been under ordinary circumstances. My mother liked to keep me home at night, as much for companionship as anything. My dad so often worked late at the store. Aunt Grace had a social life of her own. I was the only child at home. My older brother had moved away to take a job in Providence. My sister had married young and gone to live in Vermont. It's the lot of the youngest to be clung to and fussed over. Except that night, I got lucky. Old Mrs. LeWitt went on the rampage for her medicine.

BLACK DUCK

"FOR GOD'S SAKE, CAN'T SHE WAIT UNTIL morning?" I heard my father bellow in the front hall. It was past ten o'clock. My parents had already gone to bed. He was downstairs in his pajamas. Dr. Washburn was at the door.

She couldn't wait, the doctor said. She'd sent word by his office. Her nerves would fray to pieces if she didn't get her tonic.

"Hell's bells!" my father shouted. Mrs. LeWitt lived far out on the Point. Her prescription had come in late to Riley's store from Providence that afternoon. Dad had brought it home with him and forgotten all about it.

"Carl!" My mother hushed him over the hall rail upstairs.

"Somebody must go tonight," Dr. Washburn insisted. "I'd take it myself, but Mrs. Clancy's come into labor. I'm late there already. Just stopped here on my way."

I was hanging out the door of my room, ready with a solution I thought my mother would never agree to, when:

"Send Ruben," I heard her tell my father. "He's wide

awake. He can ride his bicycle down there and be back in no time. It's a beautiful night. He'll come to no harm."

"Ruben!" my father yelled up in desperation. "Would you mind making a trip to the Point at this hour?"

I was out in a flash looking over the rail. I said I wouldn't mind. No, I wouldn't mind at all.

It was the sort of spring night that makes you want to leap like a wild animal. Outside, barreling down the Point road through the crisp salt air, a furious energy rose in my bones. I wanted to ride on forever. I'd been cooped up for years, or so it seemed, following directions and doing what was right, living up to expectations that were somebody else's. You can only take orders for so long, I decided, then you've got to break free and make your own rules.

The more I thought about this, and about where I was headed at present in life, which was working for my father at the store until the end of time, the faster I pedaled. I was in a state of high mutiny by the time I got out to Mrs. LeWitt's. It took an act of pure will to put on a delivery boy's polite smile as I came up on her cabin.

I needn't have bothered.

Mrs. LeWitt, in a terrifying flannel nightdress and hair net, was in a far worse mood.

"Well, it's about time!" she shrieked. "Thought you'd never get here!" She snatched the package out of my hand and shut the door so fast she nearly took off my nose.

I laughed bleakly at myself and set off for home, going slower. The bulb in my bicycle lamp had burned out. I pedaled nearly blind at first. Then my eyes began to adjust. Pale fields floated toward me out of the blackness. Stone walls hulked and spun past. Stealthy, scuttling creatures crossed in front of me, shadows come and gone. About midway home, I glanced toward the bay rising to view on my left and there, with my new night vision, caught sight of something I might otherwise have missed.

Tiny lights were winking out on the water. Red, then white. Red, white.

I knew what they were. A boat was on its way up the east passage, sending out a code. After a bit, the lights went dark and I couldn't see anything.

I coasted to a halt to listen. A chorus of spring peepers rose from a nearby marsh. Then, as the wind shifted a bit, I heard clearly, coming up over the fields, the dull, repetitive thud-thud-thud of powerful engines driving through water. The boat's lights flashed on again. It was signaling its position every minute or so. I couldn't see, but suspected that someone on land was signaling back. In those days, houses on shore were few and far between and there was little to give direction to a boat traveling without lights under cover of dark.

I watched until I was sure where the craft was going to put in, then leapt on my bike. A few minutes later, I turned down Tyler's Lane, pedaling for all I was worth. Jeddy and I often came down this road to fish, or in our endless quest for lost pots. There was a rumor about town that the rocky beach at the end was a favored drop for smugglers. The Coast Guard must have heard this, too, because it wasn't unusual to see a patrol boat bobbing off-shore during the day, binoculars trained on the decrepit wooden dock that ran out from the beach. Now, on this perfect moonless night, I hoped the rumors were true. I wanted more than anything to see a bootleg landing close up.

I was riding down the middle of the road, where it was less chewed up, when headlights flashed in back of me. The sound of shifting gears sent me over to one side and, seconds later, a car bore down. I swerved and rode full speed into a field of tall grass, flung myself off the bike and lay still. The outline of a huge Packard raced past, going headlong for the beach. I stayed low, breathing hard, and a good thing, too, because after a minute another machine went by, a fancy touring car of some kind, followed closely by what looked like a Pierce-Arrow. I raised up for a second look and saw the big, arrogant taillights flash red. All three vehicles were out-of-towners. No one I knew owned wheels of this caliber. Peering over the grass, I saw other lights down on the beach.

The time had come to ditch my bicycle. I wheeled it to the field's edge, laid it down in some weeds and began to walk toward the water, using a low hedge along the road for cover. The closer I went, the more I could see that those three cars weren't by any means the all of it. The beach was boiling with activity. There must have been twelve or fifteen cars parked here and there, as well as trucks, a couple of delivery vehicles, even a horse van. On the beach itself, shadowy forms of men milled around in light cast by a row of headlights. They were the shore crew, silent for the most part, looking often out to sea.

Soon, the sound of a boat's engines could be heard and the wallowing form of a craft appeared out of the dark, slowly approaching the shore. I dropped to my knees and crawled up behind a pile of rocks at the far edge of the beach. What I saw next nearly stopped my heart.

Mr. Riley, owner of Riley's General Store, was standing not twenty yards away, staring intently at the incoming boat. He wore a fisherman's cap pulled low over his eyes instead of the snappy fedora he sported on visits to the store. But his double-chinned profile showed up clear in the glare of headlights. Though he was short, far shorter than my father, his meaty chest gave him the hunched look of a bulldog. More than once I'd had the impression that my father played a careful hand around the guy.

A shout came from one of the men onshore. Mr. Riley walked down to the water's edge. He was wearing city shoes and stood fastidiously out of range of the waves. The speedboat, painted an anonymous gray, sat low in the water, obviously carrying a load. It approached the dock at a fair clip, waiting until the last moment before turning and killing its engines. The craft drifted neatly wharfside and lines were tossed toward the old dock's pilings. An eager crew of men rushed out along the dock's length. With the hull pulled snug, unloading began.

Wooden cases from the boat's hold were lifted and passed along a chain of human hands down the dock and up the beach to the back of a waiting vehicle. The work went swiftly and largely without sound, except for grunts and occasional bursts of laughter when a heavy crate slipped or caused someone to lose his footing. Through the gloom, I picked out some men I knew from town. Henry Crocker, a local farmer, was there, along with Reg Blankenship, who raised hogs up the river. There was Horace White, a mechanic in the gas station at Four Corners, and Tony Rabera, a handyman and gardener for summer folk who needed upkeep on their vacation houses.

In all, some twenty men labored to bring the cases up the shore. As each vehicle was filled, it drove off into the night and another truck or van or a fancy roadster backed up to the feed line. Like a silent film, the action played in front of me: the frantic movement of the shore crew, the flicker of headlights coming and going.

The hour when my mother would have expected me home had now come and gone. I knew I should leave, but I could not. A quarter hour went by, then another. Finally, with more than half a hold of cargo still on board, an ocean swell came in that caused the gray-hulled boat to roll and crash against the dock. Work halted while boat lines were untied and cast off. With a roar of engines, the skipper began the process of moving the speedster around to the other side of the dock, where it could be in the lee and more protected from the surge.

All this took time, and at last I saw no way but that I must go. I crawled backward from my rock hiding place until I came to the edge of a field and could slide into its bushy shadow.

From there, I felt safe enough to gaze back once more at the activity on the water. The rumrunner craft was in the process of approaching the dock again. The wheelman was a young man, dark and dashing as a pirate, it seemed to me. He revved the powerful engines, idled them and, with an expert hand, allowed the boat to drift into position. As it swung around into the dazzle of headlights, I caught sight for the first time of the ship's name, painted along the starboard bow.

Black Duck.

A second later, the boat swung away. The dark captain brought the bow into the wind, revved up once more and cut his engines. Across the suddenly peaceful water I heard him give out a full-throated laugh of satisfaction. Then the chain of men on the dock began to reform for another round of unloading. With all eyes turned toward the water, I chose this moment to sneak away up the dark lane.

THE SECRET

MY MOTHER WAS AT THE DOOR WHEN I CAME in, but I was ready for her. I told her my bicycle lamp had burned out, that I'd been forced to walk a good part of the way home. Somehow, she believed me and I escaped to my room, where I lay awake, in a haze of disbelief. The *Black Duck*. At Tyler's dock!

She was half phantom, known all over Narragansett Bay for her daring runs and yet rarely glimpsed by ordinary folk. Her skipper was too smart and her crew too skilled. She'd eluded the Coast Guard and the Feds for years, and made a laughingstock of local police who tried to track her movements.

Cornered against some dark beach, the *Duck* gunned her big engines and roared to freedom, leaving pursuers to wallow in her wake. If, by some fluke, she was caught carrying goods and ordered to halt for inspection, a dense cloud of engine smoke would erupt from her exhaust pipes and she'd speed away behind it into one of the hundreds of coastal inlets known to the crew.

They were local men from local families with a need to make ends meet during hard times, different altogether from the big-city syndicates that were beginning to bully their way into the business at that time. Many folks quietly cheered them on around their supper tables, proud that one of their own could outsmart both the government and the gangsters. At Riley's store, I'd listened in on more than a few back-aisle conversations.

"Heard the *Duck* was up to Fogland last night, making a drop," I'd hear a fisherman say, shaking his head in what should have been disapproval but sounded more like supressed glee.

"That so?" a friend would reply, and several other men would suddenly materialize and gather round to hear the story.

"Yup. The Coast Guard picked up a tip that she was bringing in a load of hot Canadian whiskey from an outside rig. They'd staked out three cutters up there waiting for her, and guess what?"

"She got away!"

"She did. Dumped her goods in the bay and got clean away. Led 'em on a wild-goose chase up the east passage."

"Oh, Lord, I wish I'd seen it."

"You could'a heard it if you was up there onshore. The C.G. had a spotlight on her and was firing across her stern. They ordered her to stop, but it didn't do no good. She turned on the juice and disappeared."

"She does nearly forty, y'know."

"I heard she's got a steel-plated hull."

"Her skipper's out of Westport, somebody said. Making money hand over fist."

"He's out of Harveston, I know it for a fact. And he's not just in it for himself, they say. He gives from his profits to local families in need."

"Is that so?"

"I heard it was."

"Somebody you know?"

"Me? No. I don't know who it is."

Nobody knew who her skipper was. Or nobody would own up to knowing. And now I'd seen him. I'd watched him at work in all his swagger and bravado. My first thought, tearing home on my bike that night, was that I couldn't wait to tell Jeddy.

Only later in my room, thinking back to the men on-shore, men I knew and respected and who knew and trusted me, I began to have second thoughts. Jeddy was my friend, but there was so much at stake. Not least, there was my own father, the manager of Riley's store. I wasn't sure what Mr. Riley was doing on that beach, but I thought it best for my dad if no one heard his boss was there. Chief McKenzie was breathing fire to put a stop to the *Duck*. Jeddy might swear he'd never tell him, he might truly believe we could keep a secret between us, but he loved his dad and stood up for him, and I knew how easy it would be to make a slip.

Newport Daily Journal, December 31, 1929

BLACK DUCK TRIPLE SLAYING UNAVOIDABLE, OFFICIAL DECLARES

FAIR WARNING TO HALT WAS GIVEN

NEWPORT, DEC. 31—The Coast Guard cutter that fired on the Black Duck last Sunday, killing three men, gave a clear signal for the vessel to stop and surrender according to D. W. Hingle, commander of the Newport Coast Guard Station. The patrol boat opened fire with a machine gun after the Black Duck veered and attempted to flee.

"The loss of life is sad but was unavoidable," Hingle said in a statement last night. "The laws of the United States must be maintained. The smugglers defied the government officers and took their punishment. They have no one to blame but themselves."

The Liberal Civic League has asked for further investigation, and questions of negligent homicide have been raised by state residents who charge the Coast Guard with being "out of control" in their pursuit of smugglers.

"This was murder, pure and simple," said Henry Borges, of the League. "The crew was unarmed. Bullet holes are stitched down the side of the pilot house. There is no evidence that any 'fair warning' signal was given."

The dead are Alfred Biggs and William A. Brady of Harveston, R.I., and Bernardo Rosario of New Bedford, Mass. The sole survivor, Richard Delucca, also of Harveston, is in Newport Hospital, being treated for a gunshot wound to the hand.

The Interview

IT'S AMAZING THE COAST GUARD EVER caught up with anybody back then, David Peterson says to Mr. Hart. *The smugglers could run circles around them in their souped-up fishing boats. It must've been frustrating.*

It was, Mr. Hart agrees.

They're in the kitchen for another round, the third day of their interview, which is taking on a life of its own. David didn't even need to knock when he arrived this morning. Mr. Hart's door was wide open.

I read that the Coast Guard was supposed to give fair warning to suspected rum-running boats before they could shoot, David says. *Blow a horn or shoot off a warning gun. They had to catch the crew with smuggled liquor on board or they couldn't arrest them. I guess that's why the bootleggers were always dumping stuff overboard.*

Mr. Hart gazes at him thoughtfully, as if he's taking his measure. *You sound like you've been doing some research.*

I went to the library after we finished here yesterday. Found another old newspaper article, David says.

He doesn't reveal that he's been reading up on the *Black Duck* shooting in particular, which he's begun to realize was a big deal back when it happened. People were outraged. They wanted the Coast Guard investigated for murder. The case never went anywhere, though. Two weeks after the event, the Coast Guard was cleared by a federal grand jury of all wrongdoing.

None of this can David discuss with Mr. Hart. The ground rules for this interview have been established, though nothing has been stated outright. They are: Don't Ask and You May Be Told. The old man is especially wary of questions that attempt to connect him personally to the *Black Duck*.

Don't believe everything you read in the papers, he says now. *There's usually a world of difference between what's reported and what probably went on. Behind every story there's another story.*

David nods. He's aware that people often don't agree with how the news is reported. His father cancelled his subscription to the *Providence Journal* after reading an editorial about toxic weed-killers that sent him into a rage.

I'm not paying another cent for this birdbrained newspaper! he'd yelled. *Next they'll be calling for a ban on mousetraps!*

Whatever happened to the *Black Duck* out there in the fog, the "murk" as Mr. Hart calls it, has been further eclipsed by the passage of time. Most people from that day have died. There's no way of getting back there for a clear view.

Or is there?

You remind me of Jeddy somehow, Mr. Hart says suddenly, his blue eyes taking on a more friendly gleam. *It's easy to talk to you. Jeddy and I could be together all day and never be tired of it. Like this.*

Thank you, David says. He's begun to feel warmth for the old man in return. His manner is brusque, but he is honest and direct, and has an offbeat sense of humor that David really enjoys. Ruben Hart would have made a great friend if only he'd been born seventy years later.

You know, we don't always intend to do what we do, Mr. Hart announces suddenly.

Such as?

I didn't mean to get into what I did, and I know Jeddy didn't, either. He had a good heart. It was the times.

David nods, but he's lost. Whatever Mr. Hart is talking about—some betrayal is what it sounds like—must come up later in the story.

The old man sighs, leans back in his chair and by mistake knocks into a cardboard milk container on the counter behind him. David leaps and rescues it before it goes over.

Whoa! That was close. Shouldn't this be in the fridge?

The counter is crowded with other things, too. Greasy plates, unwashed glasses, a stack of sticky pots and pans. It looks like the wife is still away. Mr. Hart has been cooking for himself and not bothering to wash up.

When's your wife coming back?

When she can.

You must be missing her.

I'm doing all right.

Where'd she go?

North Carolina.

You didn't want to?

Mr. Hart shakes his head. *Wasn't invited. I never am when she visits down there.*

Well, go on. So the Black Duck *came in at Tyler's. What happened next?*

What happened was that Jeddy and I couldn't leave well enough alone. We were curious, you know, where that body might've gone.

Of course, David says. *Who wouldn't be?*

ABSENT FROM SCHOOL

I WASN'T THE ONLY ONE TO TAKE HEAT FROM my dad after we found the body on Coulter's Point.

The next day, Chief McKenzie lowered the boom on Jeddy so hard that it looked as if he'd never have another afternoon off in his life, not for lobster-pot hunting or anything else.

"I've got to get a job," he told me when we met on Monday for our walk into town to the school. "My dad said I've got too much free time on my hands and it's leading to trouble."

"What trouble? That we found that stiff?"

"No. I don't know if it's even about that. He said I'm too old to be hanging around on beaches. If I want to make money, I should get a real job."

"How about working at the store with me?" I said. "I could ask my father if Mr. Riley would hire you. You wouldn't make that much, but we could do it together."

Jeddy shook his head. "Dad already signed me up to start next week at Fancher's chicken farm. I'll be mucking and plucking and watering the flocks."

"You won't make anything there!"

"I know."

"Isn't that where your dad worked one time?"

Jeddy said it was. "That's how he got me the job."

We walked along in gloomy silence. Chicken-farm work was dirty and smelly. There seemed to be nothing more to say in the face of such a blow. Jeddy's fate looked sealed even worse than mine. I felt so bad for him that I almost let loose and told him about the *Black Duck*, if only to cheer him up. But we were passing the police station across from Weedie's just then and a knot came in my throat and I kept quiet.

We were almost to school when I thought of something else I could bring up.

"So, about that body, what do you guess happened to it?"

"I don't guess, I know. It got took," Jeddy said. He was still sore about the whole thing, I could see.

"Well, I know that, but the question is, why?"

"My dad told me not to talk about it."

"Oh, come on," I said. "My dad told me that, too. But we've got to talk about it. That's the most interesting part, that they told us not to talk about it."

"My dad said we could get in hot water by sticking our noses in," Jeddy said. "I think it's big-time mobsters fighting with each other."

I nodded. "Could be. The thing I keep wondering about is *how* the body got took. No way you could get a boat in at low tide. And there was no mark on the beach. It's like it somehow got lifted."

"Lifted?" Jeddy said. "You mean like lifted up?"

"Yes."

Jeddy frowned. "I don't see how."

"You don't?" I already knew where this was leading.

"Well . . ." He gazed at me. I could almost see the flash go off in his brain. He was remembering the far-off drone of a motor across the bay, the glimmer of silver wings in the sky.

"That plane we saw!"

"Right. If it had pontoons, it could've landed out in the water. Those seaplanes draw less water than most boats."

"But it was windy that day. They're no good in the wind."

"The wind went down, remember? It was almost calm by the time we got back there. A plane could've coasted in pretty close. Somebody could've got off and grabbed the body and gone right back up. Wouldn't have taken more'n a few minutes."

"Might've been the Coast Guard," Jeddy said. "They've got seaplanes."

"The Coast Guard doesn't go around stealing bodies. If they pick up a body, you hear about it."

"I guess it was somebody else, then. The only thing is, how would they have known where the body was? We were the only ones that knew about it. That plane would've needed somebody to tip 'em off where to land."

"I guess somebody *did* tip 'em off."

Jeddy paused and looked over at me. "Charlie's got a radio in the station," he said.

I nodded. "Remember how he took an ice age to get to your house?"

"And he didn't want us going back on the beach."

"Your dad wasn't too happy we were there, either," I reminded him.

That brought us to a standstill. Neither one of us wanted to make a guess as to what it might mean. I waited to see which way Jeddy was going to jump, whether he'd do what his dad wanted and shut up, or stick with me.

"Well, I think it's unfair," he said, at last. "We found that body and we should be able to know what happened to it. They can't treat us that way, keeping us out of everything."

"You're right!" I said. I pounded him on the back.

"If a plane came in there, it was in broad daylight. Somebody must've seen it or heard it," Jeddy went on. "Who lives down around that beach?"

"Nobody. It's too far out. Except there's old one-eye, Tom Morrison. He's got a shack on the salt marsh behind the dunes."

"That crackpot. I heard he eats raccoons."

"I heard he's got a raft and poles around all night hunting blue crabs," I said. "How about if we go down and pay him a visit?"

"Good idea."

"Soon," I said.

"Yeah, I'm for it."

"Before he forgets. He's that old."

"All right with me."

At this point, we entered the school. And we were proceeding with the most dutiful intentions across the front foyer toward our classroom when the earsplitting clang of the day's opening bell burst over our heads. This was a brand-new electrical device, hooked up that fall to replace the principal's old hand bell, and we nearly jumped out of our skins. But then, as we were recovering, we looked around and noticed something.

Absolutely no one was in sight.

The front hall was empty. So were the corridors. All the students and the teachers were inside their rooms, and the principal had gone back into her office.

"We're late!" Jeddy whispered ecstatically.

"Too late!" I crowed with delight.

A crafty look came into Jeddy's eye. "I'm beginning to wonder if we were ever here," he whispered.

I shook my head solemnly. "I didn't see us."

Without another word, we turned and ran back out the school door, and I remember how the early spring sun beamed down our backs as we hightailed it in glory across the fields toward the shore.

TOM MORRISON

WHAT JEDDY AND I KNEW ABOUT ONE-EYED Tom was what everyone in town knew: that as a young man he'd been a good fisherman. He'd had a boat and a crew and the kind of rugged strength it takes to pull a living from the sea.

But the sea has a way of breaking down even the best. One gusty afternoon, a wave swept Tom's first mate overboard, and he sank and disappeared before Tom could reach him. A few years later, a storm came up and smashed Tom's boat into the rocks, and he had no money to replace her. Then he went to work as crew for others, but a boat hook caught in his eye one day and tore his face so badly that he had to quit working.

After that, according to the story, his moods turned foul. The word went around that he brought bad luck on board a boat, and even when his face healed, no one wanted to hire him. Then his wife left him for another man, and he was forced to sell his house. And so he had retreated, alone, far out on the Point, to a shack that had once housed hens by the side of a salt pond.

From then on, he'd kept away from humanity and rarely come into town. Jeddy and I had caught sight of his gaunt figure in the distance during our treks around Coulter's Point. Neither one of us had spoken to him, though, or dared to follow the sandy footpath that led back to his shack, as we were doing now.

Tom was nowhere in sight when we arrived. We skulked around a bit. The whole place was in a shambles, overgrown with weeds and pond brush, scattered with old tins, rusty tools, broken bottles and the like. The house was actually a pair of coops nailed together, and badly so, for one side had taken to leaning far over on the other, which was itself listing at a dangerous angle. It looked to us as if a hurricane had been through, and perhaps if you thought of what life had served up to poor Tom, you could say he'd weathered more than one.

If he was still around.

A half hour later, we were about to give up and head back toward the beach when the crunch of footsteps came from the bushes. An elderly dog staggered into the yard, followed by an old man carrying a long-handled net bristling with crabs. He halted and looked us over with one rheumy eye. The other was a whitened disk in its socket.

"Hello, Tom!" I managed to call out.

This brought a second suspicious glare. Jeddy weighed in with, "We're here to ask you something, if it's not too much trouble."

Under its gray bush of beard, Tom Morrison's chin made a chewing motion, as if he were mulling this over.

Then he walked toward the house, urging his moth-eaten mutt along. He propped his net against the stoop, where the crabs rattled their claws and scrabbled together, still very much alive.

"It's no trouble of me!" he called at us. "It's trouble of you t'come all the way here."

He sat down against the chicken coop door and pried off his boots. Gruff as he was, we could see he was curious about why we were there. He was throwing us half-glances and muttering to himself. After a bit, he motioned us across the yard to sit down near him on a mound of clam shells.

"This here's Viola," he said, in a somewhat more friendly tone. The dog thumped her tail.

She was about the most beaten-down dog I'd ever seen, and so stiff-jointed, she had to circle around four or five times before her old legs would agree to let her down on the ground. But she had a gentle face and a sweet way about her. When she'd settled, Tom reached out and stroked her with a wide, rough hand.

"Hello, Viola," Jeddy said, leaning forward to give her a pat. She thumped her tail again. Then we got down to business.

"What we want to know," I began, "is if a seaplane came in here a few days back. Not here, I mean, but off the beach out there. It would've had pontoons and made a good amount of noise, and we wondered if you saw it."

Tom stared at me out of his good eye. I was trying my best not to look at his bad eye, which had no pupil and bulged from his head like a peeled egg. Most people would've put a patch over something like that out of plain good manners. Tom was way past worrying about such things, I could see.

"Why we're asking is, we found a dead body there a couple of days ago," Jeddy continued, probably thinking it might help to give the whole story. "And when we left to report it, somebody stole it. And there were no signs of where it went, and no one's talking about it. We think that's fishy."

Tom stared at him. He still didn't trust us and was holding back on an answer. Something else had already answered for him, though. A fancy gold watch was around his wrist. Jeddy and I both saw it. When Tom saw us looking, he raised his arm to make a proud show of the thing.

"We sure would appreciate anything you could tell us," I said. "It was midafternoon when we were there. A bunch of seagulls was making a racket over the body."

"Doing more than making a racket," Tom replied, gazing fondly at the watch. "Having quite a banquet for themselves. Quite a banquet!" He glanced up, amused by his own words.

"But then, somebody must've come. Flown in is what we guess," I pressed him. "We came back later, about suppertime, and nothing was there. No gulls and no body."

"And no empty liquor crate," Jeddy put in. "It'd been there, washed up with the body."

Tom stared at us. "Well, I got that," he said. "After you left. There it is. Might be of use one day."

We looked where he was pointing. The crate was lying cocked up against an overturned skiff across the yard.

"So you saw us," Jeddy said.

Tom grinned. "How d'ya like my new watch?" he asked, holding up his arm again.

"We like it," I said. "It was on the dead man, right?"

"He don't care," Tom said. "He got no use for it now. Anyways, I left him his wedding ring."

"We won't tell," Jeddy said. "We just want to know about the seaplane. Did you recognize the guys in it?"

"Naw. I don't know 'em. Somebody'd been keeping a watch on these beaches, though. Been a big speedboat nosing up and down the coast all week, like it was looking for something. Then in comes the plane."

"Was it the Coast Guard?" I asked.

"Nope. Nobody I ever saw. Tough guys." He paused and sucked in his breath before uttering his next remark. You could see it was distasteful to him, something he didn't want to dwell on.

"They got machine guns," he said. "When they come off the plane there's two of 'em, and they wade ashore holding the guns over their heads. One takes and shoots the dead man. Rat-a-tat-tat. Shoots him dead again. Then they laugh. They drag him out through the waves back to the airplane, and take off."

"Where'd they go?" Jed said.

Tom shrugged. "I stayed hid. I was glad I took time to cover my tracks."

"They never saw you watching?"

Tom shook his head grimly. "They're shooting dead men, so I see they're not particular to what gets shot. Me and Viola, we stayed hid."

School being in session until 2:00 P.M., it seemed best to keep a low profile until that hour. After our talk with Tom, Jeddy and I stuck around in the yard and played with Viola, who still could fetch a stick, though it took her a while to get it back to you. Meanwhile, the old man disappeared inside his shack to heat up a pot of water to cook the blue crabs he'd caught. That was how he ate, never mind what time it was. Schedules the rest of us followed, like breakfast, lunch and dinner, night and day, had lost their pull on him. He was living free of all rules, even the most basic.

I was watching him like a hawk, I've got to say. I'd been under a heavy regime of right and wrong, good ways and bad ways, ever since I could remember, and to see one-eyed Tom out from under, cracking blue crabs at ten o'clock in the morning and falling asleep without even getting up from the table, was a sort of revelation to me.

About noon, with Tom snoring in his chair, Jeddy and I went back to the beach and lay around out of the wind in the dunes. Unless you're a seagull, there's nothing comfortable about an open beach on the Rhode Island coast in May. Keeping our heads down, we ate our school lunches. Afterward, for sport, we crawled around looking for terns' eggs in the dune grass. It was too early in the season for turtles to be laying.

"Well, that's the end of it, I guess," Jeddy said as we rested after these activities. We were back on the subject of the dead man. "The guy was in deep with some bad characters and got shot. My dad is right, it was rumrunners and we probably don't want to know any more about it."

"Makes you wonder, though," I said. "Why were they looking for a guy that was already dead? Then they shoot him again, like they can't stand his guts."

"Maybe it wasn't them who shot him in the first place," Jeddy said. "Maybe it was somebody else and they needed to prove to themselves that the guy was dead. He was probably double-crossing everybody."

"He was a high roller, that's for sure. He must've been hauling in the dough to afford a watch like that. That pipe and tobacco pouch, they're both quality, too."

There was a pause in the conversation while we looked over the dunes at a fishing rig that was chugging along off-shore. It passed the beach and went on up the coast.

"Well, you know what Marina thinks," Jeddy said.

"What?"

"She thinks Charlie Pope's gone in with a big bootleg gang. He's been acting like he's some kind of hotshot."

"She doesn't like Charlie. She put him in his place, too. Marina knows how to do that."

"She doesn't like Charlie for a good reason," Jeddy said. "Don't tell anybody, but he tried some funny stuff on her."

"What do you mean?"

"She was walking home from the bus after school one day, and he pulls up in his car and says for her to get in, Dad wants to talk to her. So she gets in, and he starts driving to Harveston. When she asks him what's going on, he says 'nothing,' he just wanted to get to know her better."

"That's crazy. He's ten years older than her."

"I know. So she says to take her home. He says he will, but he has an important errand up the road, and will she just sit tight until it's done? Police business, he says. So, she says all right, and when they get to Harveston, he goes into some place by the train station, and comes out ten minutes later with a couple of guys in suits who shake his hand and drive off in a fancy car.

"When he got back in the car, Marina asked who they were. He told her not to worry about it, they're old friends. He was showing her how important he was, I guess. Then, on the way home, he starts up with her again and pulls into a field off the main road."

"That scum. What's gotten into him?" I was getting furious listening to this. "What'd Marina do?"

"She got out and started walking."

"He didn't touch her, did he?"

"He tried, but she got out too fast. She went back to the main road and walked, and he was driving along beside her, begging her to get in, that he wouldn't do anything, but she didn't trust him and kept walking. Then Emma Pierce came along in the Harveston taxi, and Marina flagged her down and got away. She came home okay."

"She told you all this?"

"She didn't want to. She would've kept it a secret like she does everything. But I saw her getting out of Emma's taxi up the road from the Commons. She was afraid I'd tell Dad about seeing her, and that he'd ask her about it. I had to swear not to say anything. Dad would go through the roof if he knew what Charlie did."

"I wish she'd tell him. Charlie'd get fired!"

"That's what I said, but Marina said, 'Don't tell,' because Dad is funny about stuff like that and he might blame her."

"Blame her! He wouldn't." All this was giving me a new view of what it meant to be a girl with a pretty face.

"He might. He gets mad if he sees anybody looking at her the wrong way. Last summer, when Elton White came over and sat on the porch without even asking, Dad said it was Marina's fault, that she was leading him on."

"Marina wouldn't do that!"

"I know. He wouldn't listen to her, though. He told her he'd have his eye on her from then on."

At this point, we were interrupted by the sound of a motor out on the water, and we peered up over the dune again. A high-powered rig was coming in to the beach. We flattened out and watched.

THE KILLERS RETURN

THE BOAT WAS A DOUBLE-ENGINE SKIFF BUILT
for speed, we could see that right away. Three men were
on board, including the wheelman, who was a good skipper because he knew how to bring the skiff in close to a
rock that stuck out from the beach, and turn her so his
two passengers could jump off. The tide was low and nobody got wet. We watched, hardly breathing, as the two
walked down the rock to the beach. We were hardly
breathing because they were carrying machine guns.

"Oh, Lord, it's them back again," Jeddy whispered.
"What're they up to?"

"Looks to me like they're going to see Tom," I said.

That was it, all right. They passed close by our hiding
place in the dunes and walked in toward his shack on the
marsh. One was a big guy in overalls and suspenders, and
a broad-brimmed hat. The other wore a fisherman's cap
and was smaller but sharper-looking. From the ugly set of
their mugs, we knew they meant business. We sat tight
after they went by. A couple of minutes later, we heard
yelling and a yelp from Viola. I couldn't lay low anymore.

"I'm going to go see what's up."

"I will, too," Jeddy said.

We crept toward the pond, staying off old Tom's path. We hadn't gone very far when we heard a machine gun go off, one short blast, then one longer one.

Jed dropped down and wrapped his arms around his head. "Oh, no, no," he moaned. "They've gone and shot Tom."

I was scared, too, and I crouched down beside him but with my eye on the road. Pretty soon I saw the two thugs come hustling back toward the beach, their guns across their shoulders. Out on the water, the wheelman must've been watching for them, because the speedboat was already moving toward shore to pick them up. The two went out on the rock the way they'd come, and the skiff hovered alongside it and they jumped on board. Then the wheelman buttoned her up and roared off, passing outside West Island. It looked to me as if they were headed to Newport.

As soon as the boat was far enough away so they wouldn't spot us, Jeddy and I got up and ran like madmen to Tom's shack. We expected to find him sprawled in the yard, but there he was! We couldn't believe our eyes. Old Tom was all right, and he was sitting outside his door, bent over a little but still very much alive.

We yelled and jumped for joy. "Tom! We thought you were killed! Oh, Tom! You're all right! Who were those guys? What did they want?"

He didn't answer and he didn't look up. We couldn't figure out what was wrong.

When we came a little closer I saw he had Viola in his arms. A sick feeling came into me and my knees got weak. I stopped running and let Jeddy go ahead. Tom had his face in Viola's fur. He was holding her and rocking her back and forth in a sort of agony. Jeddy got down and put his hand on Viola's neck and it came away red.

Tom was talking to her when I came up. "Old dog, oh, old dog. Don't you mind, don't you mind," he was saying. He kept rocking her, as if it would bring her comfort. There wasn't anything that would've done that, though. Her eyes were open but the light had gone out of them.

Jeddy turned to me with a terrible face.

"They shot her," he said. "They've gone and killed Viola."

It was quite a while before we could gather ourselves enough to think of what to do next. I felt numb all over and Jeddy was just as bad, I could see. One glance at Tom Morrison was enough to break your heart. He wouldn't let go of Viola, kept rocking her and whispering into her ear. When a half hour had passed and he was still at it, we began to worry that this was the final catastrophe in his life that would drive him over the edge forever.

"C'mon, Tom. Let's get up," I said. "You've got to tell us what happened."

"I believe I'll just sit here with her awhile longer," he answered in a quavering voice.

So we sat on with him, and in the end I saw it was a wise thing to do. Viola was killed in a most sudden and horrible way. She was dead as dead could be, but all around us nature was carrying on. The southwest wind began to drop, as it often will on a spring afternoon. The seaweed smell of the beach drifted in on it, along with the familiar cries of gulls. The sun went in and out of clouds, progressing toward the horizon. Gradually, Jeddy and I began to feel steadier, as if the sea and sky and birds and whatever else was out there were wrapping themselves around old Tom's place, just as he was wrapped around Viola, and telling us "don't you mind, don't you mind."

Tom must've felt some peace come into him, too, because at last he put Viola down and got to his feet. He went out back of his shack and came back with a couple of shovels. He handed one to Jeddy.

"She'll need a resting place," he said. "The sooner the better."

He showed us a shady corner of the yard where Viola liked to lie on hot afternoons, and we took turns digging. When the hole was deep enough to take her, Tom carried Viola across to it, and put her in just as she was, and covered her up after one last look.

"Take her to the good place. She were the best of dogs," he said, nodding up at the sky, as if to give God the go-ahead.

Then we bowed our heads to say a prayer for her in our thoughts, though by this time I wasn't in a very prayerful mood. I was over my shock and getting angrier by the minute. The only thing I could think was that I was going to catch up with the two bums who'd killed Viola and make them pay for it. But first I had to find out from Tom why they'd come.

"They was looking for something," he said.

It was getting on toward late afternoon by the time he came around to giving us this information. Jeddy and I had been pressing him to tell us what happened, and he kept putting us off. The thugs had been in his shack and torn it apart on the inside. His chair and table were overturned, the bed mattress was on the floor, the stove pipe was pulled out of the wall. We helped him put things to rights, swept up some broken dishes and pounded out a dent in his big boiling pot. He owned very little and it didn't take us long. How any man could get by with so few possessions, I don't know.

Afterward, we told him we had to go. Marina would be expecting Jeddy home. I should've been at the store long ago for my afternoon job. I knew I'd have to tell my dad some story about being kept after school, which was going to take some doing since I hadn't been back to the place all day. Jeddy asked Tom one more time what those tough guys had wanted. Finally he answered: "They was looking for something."

"For what?"

Tom held up his arm. The dead man's gold watch was gone.

"Grabbed it right off me," he said. "But that weren't it."

"They wanted something else?"

"The big one kept yelling: 'Where's his wallet? We know you took it.' I told 'em over and over there wasn't no wallet. I didn't take nothing else. He got real mad, went in my shack and kicked stuff around. Finally the little one stuck his head in and stopped him.

" 'C'mon, Ernie, he ain't got the ticket. Let's get outta here.' So the big one comes out. But Viola was standing there and he tripped over her. That made him mad again and he up and shot her."

I couldn't believe it. "But why?"

"There's no why to it. He tripped, that's all. Wasn't Viola's fault. She was just standing there." Tom shook his head helplessly. "He up and shot her, and then they took off. Whatever that ticket is, I don't know. I didn't take nothing else. Only the watch. They could've had it back without grabbing, too. Just ask, that's all. They didn't have to . . ."

He was overwhelmed and mopped his eyes. "I never thought somebody could do a thing like that," he went on in a ragged voice. "Kill an old dog because you trip over her. I just never thought it."

"We're going to report it," Jeddy said. "Don't you worry, my dad is going to know about this."

Tom nodded. You could see he didn't care one way or the other. What was done was done, as far as he was concerned. Viola was killed and that was the end of the story. All the way walking home that afternoon, I felt bad for him. I was also afraid of what would happen when Jeddy's father found out how we skipped school that day.

"Do you have to say anything yet?" I asked Jeddy. "Tom doesn't care. Maybe we should keep today to ourselves."

"Nope, I'm telling him," Jeddy said, determined as he could be. "I've got to. It's police business, two guys coming in, roughing up old Tom and shooting his dog. It's my responsibility to tell."

"Well, take me out of it," I said. "You can say you were down on Coulter's by yourself."

Jeddy shook his head. "I'm telling the whole truth about both of us," he said.

"Why, when there's no use in it?" I was getting hot under the collar.

"Because it's right. It'd be a lie any other way."

"It'll be all right for you maybe, but for me, it won't be," I told him. "My dad is going to take it out on me. He's a stickler for stuff like this. It's not just school. I should've been at the store all this time. The store is *my* responsibility."

"Well, I'm sorry about that, but I can't help it," Jeddy said. "This is police business."

"I didn't know you were working for the police," I yelled at him.

"I didn't know you were such a liar," he yelled back.

After that, we were too mad to talk any more. We walked up the road staring straight ahead, and if thoughts could freeze air, there'd have been a big block of ice between us.

As soon as I could, I veered off and took a shortcut across the fields toward my house. I didn't know what I'd say to my father that night. Then, as it turned out, I didn't have to say anything because he'd been in Worcester all day picking up supplies, and nobody missed me at the store. They must've thought I went with him.

Also, by pure luck, I met Mary Marquez, who was in my class, on my way back and she gave me the assignments for the next day. I got home and did my schoolwork first thing, which impressed my mother. So, for the time being anyhow, everything came out all right for me.

Only, late that night, I woke up and thought about Tom Morrison in his shack behind the dunes. I thought how he must be missing Viola. Here was a man who'd had big dreams once, but who'd been beaten down to the point where he wasn't asking for anything anymore. All he wanted was just one old dog and a shack by a pond. Then look what happens.

Life wasn't being fair to Tom, that's what I decided. It kept taking things away from him. He was trying to live it the best he could and, over and over, it kept taking things away.

The Interview

THE OLD MAN STOPS, LEANS FORWARD, BURIES his face in his hands.

That's enough for today.

David looks down at his notepad and discovers that, once again, he's forgotten to write anything on it.

Life not fair, he scrawls hastily while he can still remember. *Tom Morrison. Blue crabs. Thug stumbles over dog (Viola). Shoots it.*

He shakes his head at himself. He'll have to improve if he's going to be a professional journalist. Maybe he should learn shorthand or buy a tape recorder. Newpapers have started checking their reporters' research notes. They want to be sure they're getting the truth. Some phony articles have been uncovered recently, written by reporters who made things up.

I thought you said you and Jeddy never fought, David says, nitpicking. At least he can go after the old man's contradictions.

We never did, Mr. Hart answers. *Till that day.* He turns away in his chair, making it clear that he doesn't want to talk anymore. David plunges ahead anyway, a little meanly.

This time, I think you were wrong. Jeddy was right. He had to tell his father the whole truth. His dad was the police chief. A crime had been committed.

That's backseat driving. If you knew my father, you wouldn't have told, either.

David nods. Knowing his own father is quite enough to see the point of this argument.

Also, you don't know the whole story about Ralph McKenzie yet, Mr. Hart adds.

I can bet he was under some pressure to go along with things, David says. *Especially if it's like you say, that small-town cops didn't make much salary in those days. It sounds like the McKenzie family could've used the money.*

I guess you could put it down to that.

Why, was there something else?

Mr. Hart doesn't answer; the shop's closed for today.

Is it okay if I come again tomorrow? David asks. *I hope I'm not taking too much of your time. There's more here than I expected.*

My time? I've got more of that than I know what to do with.

Well, is there anything I could bring back for you? From the store, I mean? David noticed there wasn't much in the refrigerator when he put the milk in, just some kind of white soup in a plastic container. A guy that age shouldn't be living alone.

Is someone helping you with shopping? he asks.

Mr. Hart's eyes brush over him. *Someone helping me, did you say?*

Yes. It looks like you could use a hand around here, with your wife away.

The old man raises an eyebrow. *From you?* he asks, and laughs. *So, are you driving now? I mean, aside from giving out free advice to old fools like me.*

Well . . . no. Actually not yet.

A senior in high school and you can't drive a car?

Well, ah . . .

In fact, you're not in high school yet, are you? You'll be a freshman in the fall. You're in no position to interview anybody about anything. You've never even had a job that wasn't handed you by your family.

That's true, David admits, his face getting hot. *How'd you find out?*

I've got my sources. I may look slow, but I can still get around.

Sorry, David says. *That was stupid of me. I guess I stepped out of bounds.*

You did.

I'm sorry I lied about high school, too. I was afraid you wouldn't talk to me if you knew my real age.

Figured that, Mr. Hart says. *I don't mean to needle you. I'd guess you have some of the same problems I used to have as a kid. Your dad's got a big landscaping business, I hear.*

He does.

You're supposed to work there for nothing?

Well, almost nothing. He gives me a little. It's kind of taken for granted that I'll be going in with him.

87

And you want to get away from what's expected. You want to break ground on your own.

David nods. *My idea is to go for journalism. I'd like to write.*

Well, I admire that, Mr. Hart says. *Everybody should have a chance to start fresh, take possession of what's truly his. You know, I never did that. Professionally, that is.*

Why not?

The Depression came on and jobs dried up. I stayed here and took over managing Riley's store from my father. Jeddy made it out of this town, but I didn't. Seems kind of funny to me now.

Did Jeddy leave because of something his father did? Chief McKenzie, I mean, David asks.

I may get to that, Mr. Hart says. He waits a minute, then adds: *And then again, I may not. I haven't decided.*

You said you didn't start fresh professionally. But you had something else going?

I did, yes.

Which is the reason you stuck around here?

Yes, I'd say so. I've been lucky in other quarters.

Which are?

Ruben Hart gazes at him a long moment. Then, in the maddening way he has of ignoring direct questions that cut too close, he changes the subject.

If you still want to do something for me, there is one favor I could ask, he tells David.

Okay. Shoot.

There's a pair of hedge clippers out in the garage, hang-

ing high up on a hook. If you could get 'em down for me, I'd be obliged. I'd like to do some pruning around this place before the wife gets back. I was noticing this morning as you came in, it's a jungle outside the front windows.

Sure, David says. *No problem at all.* He goes to look for them.

The question about Chief McKenzie nags at him, though. Later, as he's driving home with his mother, he asks her: *Did you ever hear of a police chief in this town named Ralph McKenzie? He would've been here in the 1920s.*

She shakes her head. *Too long ago for me. There might be a record of him at the town hall.*

The next morning, on their way to Mr. Hart's, David has his mother stop by. He checks with the clerk, but finds no reference to anyone named McKenzie. There's nothing mysterious about this, however. The records on police chiefs only go back to 1930.

COCKFIGHTERS

WHATEVER JEDDY TOLD HIS FATHER ABOUT the gunmen on Coulter's Point, it didn't come to anything. As far as I could see, nobody heard about it. Chief McKenzie never went down to investigate. I know he didn't because I began keeping an eye on Tom Morrison after that.

Jeddy and I weren't on speaking terms, and even if we had been, he was working at Fancher's chicken farm and I was working at the store and there was no time for us to be together. It got to be a habit of mine that if I had an afternoon off, usually on weekends, I'd go see Tom. I'd bring him a newspaper and a pound of coffee or a loaf of store bread, something to give me a reason for the visit. We wouldn't do much, just sit around and shoot the breeze, but I got to like him and I believe he liked me.

He never complained about anything, not the weather or his lost eye or any of the bad luck that had befallen him. If you started him telling stories about his fishing days, he could be very entertaining. I asked him if he didn't want to get another dog to keep him company, and he shook his head. He said any dog that wanted to come find him, he'd take it in, the way he had Viola. Otherwise, he wasn't looking for one at this late date.

"How did Viola come to you?" I asked.

"Swam in," Tom said, his good eye brightening. He loved to talk about her. "She were a long-distance swimmer in her day. What I believe is, she come over from Newport."

"Swam over? Impossible! She'd have to go five miles or more."

"That's what I believe she did. The reason I say so, I have a friend with a boat who came across a dog swimming off Land's End over there. He didn't think nothing of it till he came to visit me one day. And he says: 'I swear if that isn't the dog I saw swimming.' I already knew she was good in the water, so I didn't doubt it. She'd swim alongside my raft while I was out crabbing, be in the water for a couple of hours and never get tired. This was a while back when she was a younger dog, of course."

After a story like this, he'd get quiet. His beard would go into the chewing motion that meant he was working something through. He wasn't a man easy in his own skin. He had days of darkness and bad humor, though he did his best not to show it. He told me once that his battles in life were as much against himself as any other demon. "Weather and women included," he added, with a wink.

He was a character, all right, and fascinating to me for his determination to follow his own path and take orders from no one, lonely as that was.

As the days passed, I wondered why Chief McKenzie wouldn't show more interest in what had happened to him, if in fact Jeddy had told his father, which I didn't doubt. But I let it ride. Tom wasn't complaining and, at that time, there was so much going on of a cloak-and-dagger nature around the area that two goons with machine guns probably didn't amount to much. Chief McKenzie soon had his hands full in another direction anyway.

A couple of gaming men arrived from Massachusetts and began running cockfights out in the woods. This was a matter of putting two long-taloned roosters together in a ring and watching to see which one would tear the other apart. It was a grisly amusement that tended to attract bad types. Soon roughnecks from all over were showing up to bet on the cocks. They were drinking and carousing and getting into fights themselves. Chief McKenzie wasn't about to tolerate that kind of behavior. One night, he and Charlie went out and broke up the party. They ended by arresting a good number of outsiders.

There was a small jail in town connected to the town hall that mostly went unoccupied. All the week after Viola got killed and all the week after that, it was full of spitting, cursing, riffraff cockfighters waiting for their court dates to come up in Providence. The judges had gotten behind with all the smuggling cases that were coming in and a backlog had developed.

People in town went by to get a look at the outsiders, then they'd saunter over and buy a soda at Riley's store and talk about it. I was hauling stock like a mule there every afternoon, building up some capital in case my father ever heard about the day I took off. One afternoon, Marina dropped by to get a few groceries and she came out back to talk to me.

"I hear you and Jed aren't getting along," she said. It'd been over two weeks by then.

I just nodded. I felt sore enough about our falling-out that I didn't want to talk about it, and anyhow, the way she looked was taking its usual toll on me. She had her dark hair pulled straight back in a ponytail that went halfway down her back. This was to show she meant business, I guess, but a few strands she didn't know about had come loose and were bouncing around on her neck. I was trying not to look at them. I could see how a guy like Charlie Pope might go after her, crazy as that was. In my eyes, and maybe in his eyes, too, Marina was a natural: beautiful without trying and without caring about it, either. That was a mistake, of course. I still had a lot to learn about girls. The truth was, she just hadn't yet met the person who would make her care.

Strangely enough, Charlie Pope was what Marina had come to speak to me about.

"Has he been over here bothering you?" she asked.

I shook my head.

"Well, he's been at Jed."

"About what?"

"The dead man you found. He thinks you and Jeddy might've taken something off the body."

"Like what?"

"A wallet."

My heart took a leap. It put Charlie in the same ring with Tom Morrison's gunmen. All of a sudden, Charlie Pope didn't seem like some small-town cop taking a few dollars to look the other way. He seemed a lot worse.

"There wasn't anything on him," I told Marina. "No wallet or ID. Only thing was a pipe and a tobacco pouch." I didn't mention the gold wristwatch. That would've brought up Tom Morrison, and I couldn't see the use of it. "What's Charlie looking for, anyhow?"

"He won't say." Marina gave me one of her extra-sharp glances and lowered her voice. "Listen, Ruben. Charlie's into some rotten business. You watch out for him, all right?"

"Does your dad know?" I asked. "Can't he do something about it?"

"He has to be careful, too. Charlie's got connections."

"What connections? Can't your dad report it?"

"He's doing what he can. You just keep an eye on yourself. And get straightened out with Jed," she added, more lightly. "It's not the same without you hanging around all the time. Anyway, you've got supper coming."

I knew she was talking about how Chief McKenzie had dis-invited me the afternoon we found the body. I'd been missing their house a lot. It felt good to know one person at least was missing me.

"Thanks!"

She flashed me that fine smile of hers and went back up front to do her shopping.

After that, I couldn't stop grinning. All the next hour, I was putting on the steam and working twice as hard as usual out of pure happiness. Mr. Riley was there on one of his visits from Boston, and he must've noticed. He pulled me aside when Dad was out of the store.

"You're getting to be a big, strong fellow."

"Yes, sir," I said, proud to be complimented but also suspicious of what he wanted.

"I could use a fellow like you. Would you be interested in taking on a job tonight?"

After seeing him on the beach at Tyler's, I had an idea already of what it might be, so I hedged. "I'd better check with my dad," I told him. "He might not want me out riding around like that."

"I believe I could fix it with him," Mr. Riley said. "If I did, what would you say to this?" He handed me a ten-dollar bill. It bowled me over.

"Well, I guess I could do a job if my dad says so."

"That's all right then," Mr. Riley said. "Your pop's a good man. Finest manager a man could have. You be down at Brown's Cove tonight at nine o'clock and there'll be another ten dollars for you. And a bit of an adventure, as well."

He gave me a wink and walked off.

I wanted to go down to Brown's, no doubt about that, but I also wanted to be sure it was all right with my father. It seemed odd to me that he'd agree, since as far as I knew, he'd kept himself clear of the rum-running business. When he came back in the store, I asked if I could speak to him. He said not right then.

Later, I tried to ask him again, but he put me off. It was a busy afternoon, with kegs of molasses and sacks of flour coming in, and egg deliveries from a couple of farms. I didn't get to speak to him in private until just before I was leaving to go home to supper.

"Tell your ma I'll be late tonight," Dad said. "You two go on and eat. I'll be home for a bite about nine."

I said I'd tell her. "There's something else," I said.

He'd been about to walk off, now he wheeled around on me. He knew what I was going to say. Later, I found out he'd been twice to talk it out with Mr. Riley, and that was why he kept putting me off.

"All right! You do what's been asked of you," he snapped, before I could even open my mouth. He was angry. "It'll be just this once."

My chin dropped a little. I didn't like the way he was agreeing to it, like he was being forced to.

"I won't do it if you say not to," I told him.

"I'm saying do what's been asked and keep it to yourself," my father repeated, as if he couldn't bring himself to mention what it was. "I'll deal with your ma when I get back."

"So, I should just ride my bike down to Brown's after supper and—"

Dad cut me off right there. "How many times do I have to say it? Now, get on home!"

I went. I had a bad feeling about what might have gone on between Dad and Mr. Riley, but it didn't last long. Twenty dollars was a small fortune to a kid in those days. The money wasn't the only thing, either. I'd known other boys, mostly older than me, who'd been hired onto shore gangs. You'd never want to ask them about it, and they wouldn't be stupid enough to boast, but there was an un-spoken awe and mystery that surrounded them and left a big impression on the rest of us. Now I was to be one of those chosen few. Whatever my father might think, that was something I wouldn't mind.

What he told my mother about where I went that night, I never asked. I know that when I got back from the job, long after midnight, there was a plate of cookies set out in the kitchen, and a note from her telling me to pour myself some milk. Otherwise, my mother never said a word to me and I never said anything to her. I'd come home safe and eaten the cookies and that was all she had to know. Which was a good thing because if she ever had found out what went on that night, she'd never have trusted my father to let me go anywhere again.

THE JOB AT BROWN'S

IT WAS DAMP OUT. DARK AND MUDDY ON THE road. A spring rainstorm had been through during the day and not much had dried off when I left for Brown's Cove that evening. I pedaled slowly. The wind was blowing into my face, which led me to thoughts of Jeddy and his cap that would never stay on. Seeing Marina that afternoon had made me homesick for him, if you can be homesick for a person. We hadn't said two words in as many weeks and had taken to walking to school by different routes so as not to run into each other.

I was ready for a change.

It wasn't Jeddy's fault his dad was who he was. When I thought about it, I could even admire how Jeddy was sticking to his guns, backing up his father in a difficult time. I knew I'd do the same for my father if it came to that.

I made up my mind to speak to Jeddy as soon as I could. We'd work it out. He'd agree not to ask me what was going on along the beaches. I'd agree not to let anything slip that he'd have to report as "police business." We'd been friends for so long, it didn't seem as if it'd be that hard.

Brown's Cove was a good three miles out of town. Before long, I knew I wasn't the only one headed there. Five or six vehicles rushed by me in the dark, driving without headlights. One of them was Mr. Riley's fancy red Lincoln. I knew it well. He parked out front of the store whenever he came down from Boston. I'd replaced the bulb in my bicycle lamp and had the beam cocked way up to spot out potholes ahead. I think Mr. Riley recognized me as he went by because an arm came out and waved just before the Lincoln disappeared into the dark. I liked that, being recognized by Mr. Riley. He was giving me a lot more scope than my own father, trusting me to do a big-time job.

I'd never been on the beach at Brown's, though I'd passed it going upriver on the Fall River boat a couple of times. It was a natural cove sheltered by a dip in the coast, a good place for a hidden landing. When I rode up, about twenty men were already there and a bunch of skiffs were pulled up on the beach, oars set and ready. The place was lit up bright as day with oil lanterns planted on the beach and car headlights shining across the sand. When I looked across the water, I was astonished to see a freighter looming like a gigantic cliff just outside the blaze of lights. It was in the process of dropping anchor. I soon found out that she was the *Lucy M.*, a Canadian vessel that usually moored outside the twelve-mile U.S. territorial limit off the coast to avoid arrest.

The way the Prohibition law was written, the Coast

Guard couldn't touch an outside rig, since it was in international waters. So ships from Canada and the West Indies, Europe and Great Britain would lie off there, sell their liquor cargos and unload them onto rum-running speedboats like the *Black Duck* to carry into shore. Sometimes as many as ten or fifteen ocean-going vessels would be moored at sea, waiting to make contact with the right runner. "Rum Row," these groups of ships were called. You couldn't see them from land, but you knew they were out there lying in wait over the horizon. It gave you an eerie feeling, as if some pirate ship from the last century was ghosting around our coast.

I couldn't believe the *Lucy M.*'s captain would be so bold as to bring her into Brown's, where any Coast Guard cutter in the area could breeze up and put the pinch on her. Nobody at Brown's seemed worried about it, though, and unloading operations soon commenced.

The skiffs on shore rowed out and took on burlap bags, which was how the liquor was cased this time, then rowed in and were unloaded by the shore gang. I was assigned to a gang of eight men that handed the bags up the beach to waiting vehicles. It was a smoothly run operation, two gangs working at once, and a bunch of skiffs rowing out and back so that just as one skiff was unloaded and took off for more cargo, another would land, stuffed to the gunnels. We worked our tails off for an hour, took a short break, then started again. The men on my gang were all good fellows, some of whom I knew from town. They weren't used to having someone as young as me on the job, and I took a lot of kidding, but I didn't care. I was happy to be there, making my twenty bucks.

Along about midnight, someone came running onto the beach, shouting: "Feds! Feds!" Right behind him came a car. It slammed on the brakes and men in dark suits jumped out with pistols. They were Prohibition agents. After them, two state patrol cars drove in, and a bunch of uniformed police officers ran onto the beach, some of whom were carrying guns, too.

It all happened so fast that I stood there, frozen to the ground. Tino, a guy I'd been working with, grabbed my arm.

"Hey, kid, hoof it!"

I took off after him. We dove behind a sand dune, then split up and crawled off into the beach grass. After about five minutes, I heard footsteps come up close to where I was lying flat out in the grass. I held my breath and the feet went away over a nearby dune. I never knew if it was the police, the Feds, or one of the shore crew scouting for a buddy. I was too scared to look.

Later, loud voices sounded from down on the beach. I crawled to the top of my dune and took a peek to see what was happening. The car lights were still blazing, and I saw Mr. Riley in a circle of police officers. Charlie Pope was there, and so was Jeddy's dad in his leather vest with his badge shining out. Mr. Riley was mad as a wet hen. His face was bright red and he was yelling.

"I bought protection!" he shouted. "I paid you for it. What're you doing here, messing up my landing?"

Chief McKenzie said something I couldn't hear that made Mr. Riley even more furious.

"Who're you working for? The big boys?" he shouted. "What'd they pay you to do this? It's my drop. I paid for it!"

Meanwhile, two men in suits who must have been Federal agents came up. They took hold of Mr. Riley on either side and snapped handcuffs on him. He tried to shake the guys off, but didn't get anywhere. They started walking him to a car. He kept glancing over his shoulder at the *Lucy M.* out in the cove. She was pulling up anchor.

"Where're you taking my cargo?" Mr. Riley yelled. He kept on yelling until they put him in the car. The last I saw of him was his fancy shoes, the ones he never liked to get wet, disappearing as they closed the car door on him.

The police had rounded up a few other members of the shore gang, handcuffed them and put them in cars. But after the Feds left with Mr. Riley, Chief McKenzie gave an order to let everyone out of the patrol cars. He and Charlie undid all the handcuffs and let everyone go.

It was beyond me what had happened. The chief drove off, followed by a caravan of vehicles, leaving the beach in darkness except for one oil lamp somebody had forgotten. Out in the cove, the *Lucy M.* was under way, heading off into Narragansett Bay. She was heavy in the water, still carrying a lot of cargo. We'd only unloaded her about halfway. I couldn't figure out where the Coast Guard was, and why no one was coming to stop her. She went out onto the bay and steamed down the coast, lights full on, as if she were the most law-abiding ship in the world.

I lay quiet for a few more minutes, then got up and found my bike in the dark. I was about to take off for the long ride home when Tino strolled up.

"Hey there, kid. I've got a vehicle in a field at the top of the lane. If you want to walk up with me, I'll give you a lift home."

"Can you take my bicycle?" I asked.

"Sure can." He was a nice guy, a dockworker who'd come all the way over from New Bedford to do this job. I'd heard him talking to the other shore workers earlier. We set off, me wheeling my bike.

"Some night, right? That's how it goes sometimes," he said.

"Does this mean we don't get paid?" I asked.

"Afraid so."

I shook my head. "I don't get it. The Federal agents arrested Mr. Riley, but then the police let everybody else go?"

"Sure they did. That was part of the deal." Tino gave a laugh. He was an old hand at rum-running, and knew the game.

"What deal?" I asked.

"The deal to put this guy Riley out of business, I guess. The way I see it, Riley thought he'd paid the Feds and the cops enough to look the other way for this landing. But somebody got to them and paid 'em a little more to take an interest."

"How'd you figure that?"

"Just from what I heard on the beach. Riley was yelling his head off at that cop."

I looked at Tino. The cop he was talking about was Chief McKenzie. I couldn't see him taking a payoff to double-cross Mr. Riley. They knew each other from town.

"The police must've gotten a tip about this landing tonight," I said. "That's why they were here. I guess they let the crew off because they were local guys."

Tino laughed merrily at this. "The police got a tip, all right, just not from who you might think. Riley's an independent operator in this area. It's no secret he's made a bundle running his own show. My bet is, somebody bigger wants to take him over."

"Who?" I asked.

"Y'don't want to ask that," Tino said. "Y'don't want to know. But if I was to make a guess, I'd say it's an outfit up in Boston. Big boys, like Riley was yelling. I hear they're on the move."

"You mean a gang?" I asked. "Like the Mafia?"

Tino gave me a look. "You didn't hear it from me."

"What'll happen to Mr. Riley?"

"He'll pay a fine and maybe sit in jail a couple of months. Nothing much. He's lucky. If it's the Boston guns he's up against, they're tough eggs. They could've knocked him off like Tony Mordello."

"Who's Tony Mordello?"

"You never heard of him? He was working the New Bedford area up where I come from. I bet this guy Riley knew who he was."

"Well, what happened to him?"

"He was running a big operation in champagne and Canadian whiskey, making money hand over fist. He'd been at it awhile, had fancy cars, a big house, furs for his wife. We were all working for him, doing real good for ourselves. Then the show falls apart. From what I hear, he got a visit from a couple of guys who wanted a piece of the action, and he told them to shove it. I guess he didn't count on who they were. One night about a month ago, Tony disappeared."

"Is he dead?"

"Nobody knows and nobody wants to ask. He went to a poker game in his evening suit and never came home. Now his operation is being run by couple of smart guys they call the College Boys, out of Boston. It's a real syndicate. They've got their own muscle."

I kept quiet after that. It was pretty clear to me who the dead man on Coulter's Beach must have been.

I told Tino where I lived. When we came to the end of my driveway, he helped me unload my bike.

"Don't know if I'll see you again," he said. "I'll probably be sticking closer to home now. It's getting too chancy on these out-of-town jobs."

I nodded and thanked him for the ride.

"Watch out for yourself, kid," he said, and drove off into the dark. Looking after him, I realized I'd never even told him my name.

Five minutes later, I was reading my mother's note and eating her cookies in the kitchen. I thought I'd handled everything fine until I went to pour myself a glass of milk and it splashed all over the table. I looked down at my hand. It was shaking like a branch in a storm.

THE BREAKUP

I SAW JEDDY ON THE WAY TO SCHOOL THE next morning. He had his cap on backward, which is what he did when he was having trouble with something. I knew him so well, I could almost tell what the trouble was. If he looked mad, it had to do with Marina or something that happened at school. If he was walking slow and looking sort of defeated, it was his dad. Jeddy was walking slow.

I came up on him and got into step.

"How's things?" I said.

He didn't answer.

I thought a little and said: "Guess what? Mr. Riley got arrested last night."

"How come?" Jeddy asked, without looking at me.

"I don't know. My dad got a call this morning. Mr. Riley's up in the Fall River jail." I was lying to Jeddy, but what I said was true. A man had come knocking at our door at 6:00 A.M. A half hour later, my father was on his way up to Fall River in our Ford.

"My dad said he's been running rum," Jeddy volunteered.

"Who has?"

"Mr. Riley."

"When did he say that?"

"A while back. My dad's had his eye on him."

"How come you didn't tell me?" I asked him. I was happy to hear the chief had been watching Mr. Riley. It put him on the right side of the law, which, after last night, I hadn't been sure of. Still, I thought Jeddy should've let me know since Mr. Riley was my father's boss.

"It was police business," Jeddy said, glancing over at me. I knew he was starting up on the argument we'd had. I didn't want to do that anymore.

"How about riding down to see Tom Morrison on Saturday?" I said. "I've been back a few times. We could go crabbing on his raft."

"Can't," Jeddy said, not looking.

"Why not?"

"I'm working at the farm on Saturday."

"How about Sunday," I said.

"I'm working on Sunday, too."

"Not all day."

"Yes I am," Jeddy said.

I gave him a hard stare. When he finally looked back at me, I said, "You don't want to be friends anymore?"

He gave a kind of defeated shrug, as if it was out of his hands.

"We don't need to talk about anything. We could just . . . you know."

He knew what I meant.

"My dad said I don't have time," he told me. His eyes slid away. I could tell that wasn't what his father had said.

"What's going on, Jed? Is it my dad? Does the chief think he's in with Mr. Riley?" It occurred to me that Chief McKenzie might believe that. My dad worked for Riley, after all.

Jeddy shook his head. "I just don't have time," he repeated.

"Because if he does, he's wrong. Come on, you know my dad's not in on it. He never would be." I stopped walking and looked over. "I might be, but never him."

I was dropping a clue, hoping Jeddy would ask me what I meant. In our good days, he would have. It was part of how close we were that we could read each other's minds. *You might be in on it?* Jeddy would've said. *What's this "might be"?* It would've given me an excuse to tell him where I'd been the night before. I was dying to be asked. I wanted to tell him about the *Black Duck.*

Jeddy didn't look at me. He kept on walking. That scared me. It seemed as if a terrible new wall was going up between us and nothing I said or did could stop it.

For a moment, I thought I'd tell him anyway. I came so close. When I think back now, I know that's what I should have done. If I'd kept to our rule of no secrets and told Jeddy what had happened at Brown's, how I'd seen his dad and all, it might've brought us together again. We could've compared notes and talked through what was happening. That might've given us a larger frame to put around things, a frame that took in a few fog banks and murky nights, not just the sharp daylight of right and wrong, which was the kind of childish picture we'd been living in up to then.

We were entering new territory, Jeddy and I, only we didn't realize it. The world was about to get tougher on us, more complicated, and there we were fighting with each other instead of sticking together as we'd sworn to do.

We came up on the school. I glanced over at him. He was looking kind of sick. I had a pretty clear idea by then what the trouble was between him and his father, and it made me angry. Chief McKenzie had no right to give orders like that. Whatever side of the rum-running business he was on—and I honestly didn't know what to think right then—he had no right to cut Jeddy away from a friend like me. Why he would do it, I couldn't understand. He knew me and he knew my dad about as well as anybody could. All I could think was, it must be a mistake.

"Listen, it's all right," I told Jeddy. "You can steer clear of me if it's easier for you. Your dad will see the truth sometime, then we'll get back together. Anyway, we'll always be friends, right? Nothing can stop that."

Jeddy didn't answer. His head was turned away and I could see from how his jaw was set that he was holding himself in. He wanted to say something, but he couldn't.

We walked along in silence for a couple more minutes. At last, he gave the tiniest nod, as if he was saying good-bye, and lit out up the road. I stopped and waited till he was inside the school before going on myself. It seemed the right thing to do to give him some room.

THE SQUEEZE

MY FATHER CAME BACK TO THE STORE FROM Fall River late that afternoon. He'd been there all day trying to get Mr. Riley out of jail, but the judge was a hard-nose and wouldn't set bail.

Right off the bat, Dad called a meeting of store employees to put the record straight.

He explained how Mr. Riley had been busted in a raid on Brown's Cove, which everyone already knew from the gossip flying around town. He said Mr. Riley would have to sit in a cell for a few days until things got worked out, and that a lawyer was on the case and he'd have his day in court. In the meantime, Riley's General Store was to go ahead with its usual business.

"Nothing has changed," Dad told us. "This store is not involved with Mr. Riley's arrest. Neither is anyone who works here. Smuggling is not part of our business, and that," he went on, sending a warning look around the stockroom where we were all gathered, "is how things will continue to be as long as I am in charge."

It was a good speech, I've got to say. For the first time, I understood why my father had been so careful not to voice an opinion, one way or the other, about rum-running. It was his responsibility to keep Riley's General Store open and on the right side of the law. Our community depended on Riley's, and he was going to see that it was well served.

I couldn't help noticing, though, that while he was giving the eye to Bink Mosher, the butcher, and Fanny DeSousa, the cashier, and even to the new stock boy, John Appleby, he never once glanced at me. This was deceitfulness of a sort, for all the time he was talking about no one being involved, he knew I'd been there on Brown's with Mr. Riley. He knew he himself had given me permission to be there.

It opened my eyes to watch my father walking the fringes of dishonesty that afternoon, though I could appreciate why he did. It was to protect the store and to give me cover, and certainly to spare my mother the worry of knowing where I'd been.

Something else began to bother me. My father didn't level with me privately, either. All the rest of that day, I waited for him to take me aside and talk to me about Brown's. I badly needed to hear his views on Mr. Riley's arrest. Was it good or bad? I wanted to tell him about Chief McKenzie being on the beach, about the charges Mr. Riley had made against him and how everyone else had been let go afterward. Was Tino right? Had Mr. Riley been set up?

Gradually, it dawned on me: Dad was never going to speak to me. He didn't want to know about my night on the beach. He even avoided being alone with me, as if he was afraid I'd embarrass him by bringing it up. If I'd been older, I might have understood. The less said the better was his old-fashioned way of dealing with a situation that had gotten out of hand, that was scaring him, maybe, because Mr. Riley had gone to jail.

As it was, I was hurt by his silence, which I turned on myself. I knew I was far from perfect, a disappointment to him as a person and a son. Now I believed I'd sunk so low that he couldn't bear even my company anymore. Cast off in this new, frightening way, I stayed out of his sight as much as I could. And that was too bad, because right then was when I could have used his help.

Charlie Pope caught up with me late one afternoon as I walked home from the store. He pulled his car over to the side of the road ahead of me and waited until I came up. Then he opened the door and stepped in front of me.

"Howdy, Ruben," he said, eyes sharp on my face.

I said hello.

"Wanted to speak to you about one small thing."

I looked at him. Ever since Jeddy had told me what he'd tried with Marina, I'd thought he was a snake. Now, just like one, his tongue flicked out over his lips, leaving a thin film of spit.

"Y'know that body you and Jed found a few weeks back?"

I nodded.

"You might be interested to hear it's been identified."

"So you found it again?"

"Never was lost. Turns out the Coast Guard spotted it from the air just after you left. Went in there in a seaplane and picked it up before we got there."

That was a lie. I kept quiet.

"He was a New Bedford man, drowned off his boat while he was sport fishing," Charlie went on. "One of those sad accidents. People don't know the power of the sea. They get a hold of some fancy boat and think they've bought the keys to heaven. Go off by themselves. Don't take precautions."

I didn't say anything. He went on.

"The fellow was a well-known businessman over there, owned a couple of restaurants. Made quite a bundle for himself. I hear his wife's in a bad state. Two little kids. You can imagine how it'd be. She believes he had some papers on him from a deal he was negotiating. It wasn't in his wallet. That turned up on the boat. Actually, one slip of paper is what they're looking for. You didn't by any chance see something like that when you found the body?"

"What kind of paper?" I said.

"I dunno, receipt-sized. Y'know, they're trying to clean up his affairs, get the estate straightened out. She is, I mean. His wife. That piece of paper would be helpful."

"Did you look in his pockets?" I asked sarcastically.

Charlie's lips twitched. He glanced down at his feet. When he glanced back up, his eyes had turned mean.

"We looked in his pockets. Yes sir, we certainly did. What I want to know, kid, is if *you* looked in his pockets."

"I didn't," I answered. I gazed directly at him. It was a bold-faced lie.

"And you didn't take anything else off that body?"

"No. I didn't even touch it. Neither of us did."

I added this to protect Jeddy. I hoped to God he'd said the same thing.

"I find that hard to believe," Charlie said. "Two kids and a body alone on a beach. First thing you'd do is search him." He was really putting the squeeze on.

"Not us," I declared. We stared at each other.

"He'd been in the water awhile," I said. "Could be this piece of paper dissolved. Or washed away."

"That'd be a shame," Charlie snapped. He got back in his car and put his head out the window. "Listen up, Ruben, you better be telling the truth. This isn't some game of hide-and-seek we're playing."

I didn't turn a hair. "Who's we?" I shot back. "You and Chief McKenzie? Or are you in this by yourself?"

He licked his lips again. "You're a smarty. I'd watch my back if I was you," he said, and drove off.

When I got home, I went up to my room first thing and closed the door behind me. I opened my desk drawer and searched around in the rear of it. The pipe and tobacco pouch were there, pushed into a corner. I brought them out into the light, feeling again the strangeness of having them in my possession. It was like holding a little piece of the dead man's life, a very personal piece that only those closest to him would have been familiar with. His wife, for instance.

Now that Charlie had told me about her, I could imagine her. She must have watched the man open his pouch and fill his pipe after dinner on many nights. What was his name again? Tony something. His young children would have caught the scent of tobacco smoke traveling up the stairs to their bedrooms. They would have gone to sleep with a peaceful image of their father in their minds. Their father, the rumrunner. Would they ever know the real story of how he'd died?

I opened the pouch to sniff the leaf myself, and with its tang in my nostrils came a sudden thought. I pushed my fingers down into the tobacco and poked around. In a second, I brushed against something, and going deeper, I pulled out a slim paper scroll. It looked like a cigarette to me, a fancy one with a fine gray-green design, somewhat misshapen from being in salt water for so long. A bit odd, yes, but a man might store a cigarette he wished to smoke later in his tobacco pouch.

It was only as I stared at this object that a faint sense of recognition arrived in my head. I put the pouch aside and began trying to unroll the thing. Seawater had stiffened it and collapsed the ends. I managed at last to spread it flat on my desk, and there, in a flash, the exotic greenish design turned commonplace. Before me lay one half of a fifty-dollar bill.

THE BILL

I LOOKED IMMEDIATELY FOR THE SECOND half. Nothing else was in the pouch. The bill had been neatly torn in half, but why anyone would do such a thing to perfectly good money was beyond me. Fifty dollars was way too much to waste that way. I wondered if it might be counterfeit, or, a longer shot, was carrying a message of some kind. After dinner, I borrowed my mother's magnifying glass from the table in the front parlor where she used it to read the newspaper.

Under the bright beam of my desk lamp, the grainy image of General Ulysses S. Grant became a series of uninteresting swirls, revealing nothing. His stern face ended at the left ear, where the bill had been torn. On the bill's back, the grand U.S. Capitol building in Washington, D.C., was sheared off down the middle. Nothing unusual there, either. I'd heard that counterfeit bills lacked the tiny red and blue threads that run almost invisibly through the background of real money. This bill had red and blue threads galore. It was real.

I gave up in disgust. Half a fifty-dollar bill was about as useless as an old bottle cap. Worse than useless, I decided, because it made you think of what you might have bought if you'd only had the rest.

If Jeddy and I had been talking, I would've showed my discovery to him and we could've had a good time making up theories about it. Instead, I tucked it between the pages of my geometry book that night, and over the next couple of weeks mostly forget about it. From time to time, it would slip out when I did my assignments. I'd reexamine it—the half was now a flattened square—and slide it back between the pages.

One day at school, I was stashing my books in my locker, getting ready to go to lunch, when I heard a voice in back of me say:

"Here, Ruben, you dropped something."

I turned around to find Jeddy holding out the piece of bill. He'd been standing back, waiting for me to finish loading my things so he could get to his locker, which still was, as it always had been, right next to mine.

"It slipped out of your book."

"Thanks." I took the bill from his hand. He watched me put it back in the book with a comical look on his face, as if to say, "Saving up to buy something with that?" I knew he was wondering about it.

"I found it in the dead man's tobacco pouch, all rolled up," I explained in a low voice. "I thought it was a cigarette."

"Too bad it wasn't," he said. "Might've been good for a smoke at least."

I laughed and so did he. We'd put in some time with

a pack of Lucky Strikes behind the McKenzies' garage not long before our breakup. For a minute we stood grinning at each other, remembering. I thought maybe that was an opening, but Jeddy turned and walked off and never said another word. My heart fell. I saw nothing had changed. He was sticking by his dad, true blue, to the end.

Mr. Riley's court date came up about midway through May. Chief McKenzie sent Charlie Pope to testify and Riley was convicted by a federal judge in Providence of "possessing and transporting liquor." He was sentenced to eight months in jail. At the store, the staff shook their heads over it.

"He got the book thrown at him," Bink Mosher said.

"You can bet there's some shenanigans behind it," Fanny DeSousa agreed. "I tell you what, I don't trust anybody anymore."

A lot of people in town were angry. Other folks who'd been brought in by the Feds under similar circumstances had gotten off with a fine. The jail sentence was unfair, most believed. There was a general suspicion that money had changed hands to put him behind bars. I even heard my father tell my mother and Aunt Grace that he'd gotten a bum rap.

"The whole thing stinks to high heaven," he said. "Somebody was out to get him, and they did. There's judges getting paid to—"

"Didn't I say so?" Aunt Grace interrupted. "Every which way you turn, somebody's asking for a payoff."

"Surely not here in town," my mother said. "Ralph McKenzie's an honest man."

They were all in the kitchen. I was listening from the top of the back stairs leading down, and I waited to hear what my father would say to this. There came a clank of dishes—they were washing up from supper—then the sound of the sink emptying.

"Carl, what've you got against him?" my mother said finally, with more impatience than she usually allowed in her voice. "We all used to be such good friends. I know Ralph's changed some since Eileen died, but who can blame him? He loved her so. I can't see why you look that way whenever I bring up his name."

There was no answer. I heard a squeak from the back door as it opened. A minute later, our old Ford was revving up and on its way out the driveway.

The Interview

I WENT BY RILEY'S STORE AFTER WE FINISHED here yesterday. You're right, there are old storage cellars still under the barn out back, David tells Mr. Hart on a hot afternoon in what has now become the month of July.

They're not the only ones, by any means, Mr. Hart answers. *You take a close look at some of the older farmhouses down near the water, you'll find trapdoors, false ceilings, closets in unlikely places. Everybody was hiding the stuff, both for selling and drinking.*

They're sitting outside in Mr. Hart's front yard, on plastic lawn chairs under a tree. David helped carry the chairs from the decrepit garage teetering on its last legs in back of the house, the same place he found Mr. Hart's moldy, calcified clippers.

It must be a law of nature, David thinks, that when folks get old, everything around them ages too: their bathrooms and kitchens, their rugs and chairs, their cars, their clothes, their pets, their books, their eyeglasses.

Just try and buy an old person anything new, though, a garden cart that actually works or a rake to replace the one with half the prongs broken off. They'll protest. They don't want it. David sees it all the time at Peterson's Garden Shop. (Despite what his dad says, he's already put in a good amount of time there over the years.) The old stuff is like family to them. You wouldn't throw out your wife just because she's lost a few teeth.

Mr. Hart goes on:

There's a house up in Harveston where a pipe runs from the beach all the way up to a big holding tank under the garage. They'd pump Canadian whiskey by the gallon up there and repackage it for delivery—you know, siphon it into olive oil tins or gasoline drums, anything to fool the Feds if they were stopped on the road.

Creative thinking, David jokes.

You wouldn't believe how creative you can get when it comes to making money outside the law.

I thought you said you weren't involved.

Like I told you, I had friends in the business. Close friends.

Well, I guess none of them has come into this story, yet, David says, slyly. *Unless you're about to get close to Charlie Pope or Mr. Riley.*

I'm not.

So there was somebody else?

A big important somebody, that's right.

Well?

Keep your cap on, you're about to meet 'em.

TOM MORRISON'S VISITOR

ONE SATURDAY AFTERNOON I WAS PEDALING toward the harbor with a package of stuff for Tom Morrison when I came up on Marina bent over her bicycle along the side of the road.

"What's the matter?" I called out. When she pointed, I saw that her front tire was flat. It had picked up some kind of steel tack and the air was already all but gone out of it.

"Where'd this come from?" I said when I got over to her. I tried to pull the thing out, but it was stuck in too deep to get leverage on.

"Look," she said, "they're all over the place here."

A great mass of tacks was lying along the roadside, and also on the other side of the road.

"I guess somebody knocked over a nail keg," was the best I could come up with.

"Oh, it's the rumrunners," Marina said, shaking her head. "They let loose with these out the back of their trucks if the cops get too close. My dad's always coming home with flat tires. Now what am I going to do?"

"Where were you going?" I asked.

"I was thinking of buying some fresh clams down at the docks, for chowder tonight. And taking a ride on a nice June day. I guess I'm headed back home, like it or not."

There was a long silence after this while she leaned down and poked at the tire again, and I looked on, thinking about possible solutions to the problem that I would never dare to mention to Marina. She had on a blue sweater and a red bandana over her dark hair, which tumbled halfway down her back. I could've stood there all day looking at her, and very well might have if she hadn't decided she'd waited long enough for me to come to my senses.

"You wouldn't give me a ride down there, would you, Ruben?" she said, standing up. "I mean, unless you're in a hurry, making a delivery for the store. I wouldn't dream of holding you up."

Something was wrong with me and I didn't know what. A year or two before, the idea of riding Marina to the harbor wouldn't have made me think twice. She would've climbed on board and we'd have been off in a minute. Now I felt as if I'd been hit over the head with a ton of bricks and received some serious brain damage.

"It isn't," I said.

"Isn't what?" Marina asked.

"A delivery. I mean it is, but . . ."

"Oh, well, in that case . . ."

"No, really . . ."

"Definitely not. You're on a job, I see that now."

"No!"

"Well, you've got a package."

"I know, but . . ."

"Ruben, no. You don't have time."

"Yes, I . . ."

"I'm just going to walk back and . . ."

"No, Marina. I can do it!" I was in a frantic state by this time.

"I've gotten you in a fizz by asking you to do something you can't," Marina said. She had that serious wrinkle between her eyes that always finished me.

"No!"

It was several minutes more before we worked things out, and she finally did sit herself down on my handlebars. This was such a nerve-racking pleasure that I couldn't think of one thing to say. She tried out a comment now and then, otherwise we rode in silence.

"Where were you going, actually?" she asked me at last.

When I said it was just to Coulter's Point to see Tom Morrison and bring him some coffee grinds, she insisted we stop by on the way back, after she'd bought the clams.

"Tom Morrison," she said. "Is he still down there in that chicken coop? I haven't thought about him in years."

"He's still there," I said. "Jeddy and I went to visit him a while ago, and I've been going by since. He's a grand old fellow. Do you really want to come? I might stay a few minutes."

Marina said she'd be more than pleased. It would give her a look at the beach, which she hadn't seen lately. So down we went, and we were quite a load on the bicycle with the addition of a couple of bushels of clams in a burlap sack and Marina laughing and balancing them on her knees.

"I'd offer you supper for all this trouble, but I guess you and Jeddy haven't patched up yet," she said. "What's the matter, anyhow?"

I didn't want to say that the real stumbling block was her own dad, so I shaded things a little.

"Jeddy wants to report everything to the police," I told her. "What I think is, you've got to pick and choose."

"Well, I'm not getting in the middle of that one." She laughed. She thought a minute and added, "You know, it's hard when your father works in law enforcement. It's like a spotlight is shining on you and you've got to do everything by the book, whether you think it's fair or not. Otherwise you'll be going against him, out in public, for everyone to see. Give Jeddy some time. He'll find a way back."

"You think he will?" I felt a little hope spring up in me.

She smiled and nodded. "You've always been friends. You can't just stop."

By this time, we were near where the dirt road to Coulter's ended and the dunes began. As we rounded a final bend, I saw that Tom Morrison had a visitor. A rowing dory was pulled up on the shore near the path that went in to his shack.

We dumped my bike. Marina put her sack of clams in a tidal pool between the rocks to keep them fresh, and we walked in through the dunes. I was jumpy about who we'd run into and kept a sharp eye out as we came up on Tom's junk-strewn yard.

One thing I wasn't expecting was a big white dog I'd never seen before that came charging toward us, barking like fury. While we were backing away, trying to talk some sense into the beast, the door of Tom's house flew open and out came Billy Brady, an older kid I knew. He'd lived in town until his family had moved to Harveston a couple of years before. Marina knew him, too. He'd graduated from the regional high school the year before.

"Sadie!" he shouted. "Hey, Sadie, stop that!"

This was to the dog, who looked to me like a white Labrador, an unusual sight around our parts. Anything purebred was. This being farm country, dogs mostly roamed free and far afield, where they met up with other dogs out of reach of human interference. All kinds of combinations of mutt would result, to the general improvement of the species, some would argue.

"Billy Brady, is this your pup?" Marina yelled over the racket.

"She is. Gives off a good alarm, doesn't she?" he bellowed back.

He strode forward to capture Sadie and drag her away from us. He was a good-looking fellow with a rowdy head of black hair who'd filled out a lot since I'd last seen him. Behind him came Tom Morrison, grinning from ear to ear. I didn't know if it was Billy or his dog that was responsible, but Tom looked the happiest I'd seen him since Viola.

Turned out it was both, and maybe Marina, too, because Tom hadn't set eye recently on a "female biped," as he was shortly to tell her. When Sadie quieted down, we made introductions, which weren't really necessary because we all knew each other, only from different walks of life. I asked Billy how he'd come to be there.

"Just keeping up with this coot," he said, jabbing a thumb in Tom's direction. "I get by every once in a while."

"Every once in a long while, you mean," Tom teased him. "Been more'n a year, hasn't it?"

Billy said it had, and he had plans to do better in the future. "My dad worked for Tom on his fishing schooner in the old days, till it got wrecked. They had some high times together from what I hear."

"We did," Tom said. "Otis Brady were one of the best. Could spot a school of blues a half mile off."

"Did your dad pass on?" I asked Billy.

"Last summer," he said. "Didn't you know?"

"What happened?"

"Well, I guess you could say he ran into some lead. The Coast Guard aimed too high."

Tom Morrison's face darkened when he heard this. "I didn't know he'd got shot," he said. "I heard it was a boat explosion that brought him down."

"That's the story the Coast Guard's been telling," Billy said, a bitter tone in his voice. "I believe different. There was an explosion, all right, but it came after, when the boat went up on the rocks. My father was shot dead at the wheel. With a machine gun."

"Was he smuggling?" Marina asked.

"Who wants to know?" Billy fired back. He knew full well who Marina's dad was.

She fixed him with her straight-in-the-eye look and said, "Billy, you know I don't work for the police."

"How do I know when you live in the same house as them?"

"Because I just told you!" she exclaimed. "You can judge me how you want."

He gazed back at her for a moment, then dropped his eyes. She'd outstared him the way she did anyone she came up against. Somehow, in the midst of his defeat, Billy Brady must've decided to trust her, because he went on to answer her question.

"My father had a couple of hundred cases on board, most of which went to the bottom when she blew up," he said. "The Coast Guard came back and fished out what was left the next day, and took it away for themselves. What I believe is, it was a setup."

"You mean the Coast Guard shot your dad for his load?" I couldn't believe that.

"Not for the liquor. The Guard was after him, all right. But some of those officers are out of control. They've started taking the law into their own hands. There's a big Boston gang that's trying to muscle in around here, and what I believe is, they ratted on my dad to one of these maniac officers, tipped him off to my dad's run that night, hoping he'd go in and shoot up the boat. Which he did.

Officer Roger Campbell, if you want to know his name. He says he didn't intend to hit anybody. Swears he was just giving 'fair warning' to stop. But everybody knows you don't fire warning shots with a machine gun into a ship's pilot house."

"Is that what happened?" Marina asked.

"It is," Billy said. "That's according to all three men who were my dad's crew that night. Somehow, those warning shots went astray. I won't say any more."

Tom looked grim. "Whether it's from the Coast Guard or the gangsters, we're losing some good men to the rum business," he said. "And good dogs, too."

Billy nodded and turned to me. "I heard about what happened to Viola. That's one reason I'm here, to see if I can get an idea of who it was that shot her."

"Who's Viola?" Marina asked. Tom brightened up at this and invited her over to see Viola's grave in the corner, where he proceeded to launch into the old dog's remarkable aquatic history. Meanwhile, Billy and I had a short talk.

"Tom says you and Jeddy McKenzie were on the beach the day the thugs dropped in," he said. "What'd they look like, if you don't mind my asking. I've got friends in the business, local guys, you know, who might've come across them."

I told him about the big mug in the wide-brimmed hat and his little narrow-eyed friend, about the machine guns they carried on their shoulders, and the speedboat with the real professional skipper at the wheel.

"They were looking for something they thought Tom had taken off a dead body that washed up. When they didn't find it, they shot Viola."

"The old buzzard didn't tell me about any dead body," Billy said. He glanced over fondly to where Tom was carrying on, at great length, to Marina. I saw his eye linger on her, too. "Any idea what they were after?"

"Tom said they kept talking about a ticket of some kind."

Billy's head jerked around. "A ticket?"

"That's right. He didn't know what they meant."

Billy gave me a slow smile. "A ticket! Well, that's their game then. Mystery solved."

"What d'you mean? What is it?"

"A ticket's what the boys call a document that proves you've got a paid contract for a shipment of liquor. Usually means a big shipment, one that's arriving on a freighter. There's a bunch of renegade operators out to hijack the cargo on these vessels whenever they can by pretending they're runners for the buyer onshore. A ticket solves the problem. The runner gives it to the freighter's captain to prove he's the right guy. The man who was shot must've been carrying one. Who was it? Somebody from around here?"

"We never knew for sure because the body disappeared right after Jeddy and I reported it. We were the ones who found it. Chief McKenzie didn't do much to follow up, but somebody told me later it might've been a man from New Bedford." I was playing my cards close to my chest.

Billy gave me a glance. "Tony Mordello."

I nodded. "That was the guy."

"So that's where Tony ended up. He was a big operator, too." Billy shook his head.

"Did you know him?"

"By reputation. No more'n that. The rumor is that the College Boys of Boston took him out. They wanted in on some of Tony's action and he wouldn't go along with them. I guess they didn't know about this other deal he'd done until after their hoodlums dumped him. Too late, they hear he's carrying this ticket. They send out a couple of thugs to look for his body."

I didn't say anything. It was making me nervous that Billy Brady knew so much about Tony Mordello and the College Boys.

He cleared his throat and stepped up closer to me. "Now listen, Ruben. There wasn't one of those documents on him, was there? When you and Jeddy found him, I mean. Nothing that would fit the description of a ticket? It could be a piece of paper, like a sales receipt, signed and dated. But a simpler thing they use is a dollar bill torn in half."

My heart skipped a beat.

"He didn't have one," I said, quickly.

Billy gave me a sharp look. "You're sure?"

I nodded.

"You could get yourself in trouble holding one of those things," Billy said.

I kept my mouth shut. A gleam was in his eye that I didn't trust.

Marina came back over with Tom then, and told me we should think about getting along if she was ever going to be home in time to cook up the clams she'd bought for supper.

"Clams!" Billy glanced at her. "You wouldn't be making clam chowder, would you?"

"Thought I might," Marina said, tossing her hair back from her face.

"How about some corn bread and a bit of bacon to go with it?"

"Could be done." She gave him one of her appraising glances, which he met straight this time with the flash of a smile.

After that, she wasn't in such a rush to get going and we stood awhile longer shooting the breeze. Sadie leaned up against first Billy and then Tom, asking for attention, which she got plenty of from both.

"Where'd you find this sweet lady?" Tom asked, ruffling her ears. He'd taken a shine to her.

"She was given me by a fellow in Harveston," Billy said, "for a good turn I did him. She's purebred white Labrador."

"I was thinking she's something special," Tom said. "Can she swim?"

"Like a fish," Billy said. "She'll go off the high-diving rock down at Walter's Point if you give her a good reason."

Marina laughed at that. "What's a good reason?" she asked.

"How about clam chowder for supper with corn bread and a ration of bacon on the side?" Billy said, giving her a wicked grin. They all broke up laughing, but I didn't. I could see Billy Brady had taken an interest in Marina and, worse, that she didn't mind.

Later, on our ride back down the main road toward home, I tried to make some bright conversation, but Marina wouldn't bite. She was mulling over something, gazing at the fields we passed with an absent expression. I'd seen her in these quiet spells before and knew better than to interrupt. We came to her bike and she insisted on getting off and walking the rest of the way by herself.

"I could take the clams and drop them at your house," I offered. "How are you going to carry them and wheel that busted bike at the same time?"

She told me no, she'd had enough free transportation for one afternoon. Then she warmed up again and thanked me for the favor I'd done carrying her to the harbor.

I said I was jealous of Jeddy for getting to have her clam chowder that night. Of all the things Marina cooked for us over the years, that was my number-one favorite.

"Don't worry, there'll be plenty of other times," she said. Then she paused, and I could see she was trying to decide whether to speak about something else.

"Ruben Hart, you'll keep quiet about where we went this afternoon, won't you?" she said at last.

I said I would.

"My father wouldn't like to hear that I've been down at Tom Morrison's talking with the likes of Billy Brady. His family's been in the rum-running business since it began."

"They might be thinking twice about staying in that business since Billy's dad was shot," I said.

Marina shook her head. "They're not, I'm afraid. Or Billy hasn't, anyway."

"What d'you mean? Is he smuggling now?"

"More than that." She leaned closer to me. "Can you keep a secret? Tom Morrison let it slip when we were talking back there. Billy's skippering liquor runs on the *Black Duck*. He was there asking Tom if they could use his place for storage."

KNUCKLING UNDER

THE MINUTE I GOT HOME FROM TOM Morrison's that afternoon, I took that torn-in-half fifty-dollar bill out of my geometry book, rolled it up the way it had been and hid it back inside Tony Mordello's tobacco pouch. Then I stuffed the tobacco pouch under my mattress and sat down on top.

A picture of the *Black Duck* coming in at Tyler's Beach rose into my mind. I had no doubt now who the dark, laughing man at the pilot's wheel had been. Billy Brady was carrying on his family tradition. The cocky skipper whose crew outran the Coast Guard night after night, who threw up ingenious smoke screens and vanished like Robin Hood into their mists, was from Harveston, right up the road. Part of me was breathless that he was somebody I knew.

But another part lay low and cautious. There'd been something a little too pushy about Billy's interest in Tony Mordello's ticket. I hadn't liked how he'd pressed me about it, and now that I'd lied about having it, I didn't want to go back. The best thing for me, I decided, was to pretend I'd never opened that tobacco pouch.

And that was what I did. As the weeks went by, the danger seemed to pass. The pouch stayed where it was, squashed under my mattress, a strange souvenir I couldn't quite bring myself to throw away. No one else bothered me about the rolled-up bill, and whatever Tony Mordello's secret deal had been, I supposed it was as dead as he was. His fabulous shipment had ended up in some-body else's hands and it wasn't up to me to worry about whose they were.

Even as one problem seemed to clear up for me, though, another was developing for our family.

With Mr. Riley in jail, my father became responsible for more than just the day-to-day operations of the store. Goods ordered from Boston, such as tobacco and dress fabric, hardware items and a line of footwear carried by the store, now fell under his supervision. He spent more time on the telephone and longer hours over the account books. He was rarely home for supper, even on weekends.

It got so bad that my mother started bringing his evening meal to the store, determined he'd have it hot and on time. Often, she'd stay if he needed help with shelving or pricing. I spent these evenings at home. I wasn't ex-pected to work overtime no matter what was happening at the store. It was a given in our family that my school-work was more important, that I'd be following in my fa-ther's footsteps soon enough, learning the business of running a store, which, in our town back then, was about as important and well-paying a job as could be found.

Being manager of Riley's store was to be a gift my father would pass on to me, and up until that spring of 1929, there seemed no reason that he wouldn't be able to. His position seemed rock solid. He was well-liked and trusted, a beacon of honesty in the community. For the most part, Mr. Riley had seen the benefit to his store of honoring this reputation, and allowed my father to maintain a buffer of ignorance about the bootlegging operations going on behind the scenes. Occasionally, the buffer was breached, as when Mr. Riley had asked me to work at Brown's and my father had felt pressure to agree, but this was the exception.

Now, with Mr. Riley absent from the store, the breach widened and the shady world of his rum-running operations began to encroach directly on my father's pristine territory. For though Mr. Riley had been arrested, his "import business," as I heard him call it more than once, continued apace. From the number of out-of-town vehicles with Massachusetts plates that began to park in front of the store, it was easy to figure that Boston's College Boys had succeeded in muscling their way in and taking charge of rum-running operations in our area.

The first thing that happened was that my father discovered a large storage "hide" for liquor on the store premises. It was dug into the floor of the barn behind the store's main building, and had probably been there a couple of years. In the past, the place had been kept padlocked, off-limits to store personnel, and if my father ever wondered what was under there, he never acknowledged it. That

June, as Mr. Riley cooled his heels in jail, my dad received a visit from a pair a husky strangers who presented him with a key to the hide and told him to make himself available on certain nights.

This, to his credit, Dad refused to do, and Mr. Riley, from his jail cell, found another man not connected to the store to do the job. Just knowing about the hide, though, confused and outraged my father. No longer could he ignore the fact that liquor was coming and going from store property. One evening, he poured himself out to my mother in the kitchen while I listened from my post at the top of the back stairs.

"Turn a blind eye to it, Carl," my mother advised. "Pretend it doesn't exist and go about your own business."

"But it does exist! It's right there under the floor."

"I know, but it doesn't concern you."

"It didn't concern me as long as I didn't know about it. Now I know, and it concerns me," my father said. His voice rose to a pitch I hadn't heard before.

"The store's the important thing," my mother told him. "You don't want to get involved in these outside activities. Mr. Riley knows how you feel. He's always seen to it you're kept out of things."

"Riley's not there to draw the line anymore," my father said. "I have bums coming in that you wouldn't believe, pressuring me to open up more storage space. I tell 'em, 'No! I won't do it!' Then I get word from Riley to let 'em have the shed, let 'em borrow the delivery van for Friday night. I know what it's for, but what can I do? It's his store, not mine. I'm afraid he'll find somebody else to run the place if I don't knuckle under."

"Oh, come, he wouldn't fire you!" my mother exclaimed.

"Wouldn't he, now, if he saw I wasn't going along? He must make ten times on smuggling what I clear in legal sales in a month. It's money, not law, that speaks loudest to him."

My mother was silent. I think she'd caught sight at last of the corner my father was in. I know I saw it. Our family was on the line, our whole way of life.

My mother spoke again, a dark voice of warning.

"Whatever you do, keep Ruben out of it."

"I'm trying, let me tell you."

"Carl, you keep him out. Trying's not good enough."

Once again, my father left the kitchen without answering. He retreated into the parlor to read the newspaper while I tiptoed back to my room.

Listening down the back stairs was something I'd done since I was small, a way of cutting through the false front of calm my parents so often laid over their real views and worries. This time, I wished I hadn't done it. I was shocked to hear my father talk about "knuckling under" to a slickster like Mr. Riley. It seemed unfair that a man of my dad's worth should be forced to go against his moral conscience in order to keep his job. That wasn't something that should be asked of anyone, I thought, and I was amazed that my mother would advise such a thing.

That night, I couldn't sleep for thinking of my father's

problems. Along about midnight, I got up, dressed and went outside to walk around. It was a windless evening, clear, with a bright moon hanging in the sky. I went up to the main road, crossed over and in a short time found myself coming up on the McKenzies' house, which I hadn't been near in some time.

Late as it was, a light shone from the kitchen. That gave me an idea. I slipped into their yard and crept close to one of the windows, thinking I'd have a little fun spying if it was Jeddy doing his schoolwork or Marina up over some sewing.

A warm glow rose from the room. The sight of the familiar wood counters, of Mrs. McKenzie's china cabinet and the black stove in the corner, gave my heart a wrench. I wished more than anything to be back inside those friendly walls. If Jeddy had been there, I'd have gone in in a minute to talk to him. I was longing for our old selves, sick of having to look the other way and pretend not to care whenever we passed in the hall at school.

There was a person in the kitchen, but it wasn't Jeddy. Chief McKenzie sat at the supper table, working by the light of a small table lamp. He'd taken off the leather vest he wore in his official police capacity, and rolled up the sleeves of his shirt. I took a moment to figure out what he was doing. Knowing what I did about the scrimping that went on in that house, it was about the last thing in the world I'd ever have expected: he was counting money.

There was a lot of it, stacks of bills piled up neat as you please. The chief was working over them slowly and methodically, the way he did everything he put his mind to, from police files to household accounts. No one would ever accuse Ralph McKenzie of neglecting his duties, whatever else they had against him. He didn't like error or failure, and kept strict control to avoid it.

I watched him lick his finger, count out a number of bills, take up a pencil and make an entry in a book. He tucked the bills into a white envelope, sealed it, wrote a name on the front. He put the envelope aside, and started over again, counting more bills, recording them. I was too far away to read what he was writing on the envelopes, but I could guess: they were names.

I knew about payrolls. My father paid the store staff weekly using identical white envelopes. Chief McKenzie was doing the same, except that the amount of money at his elbow was far more than my father had ever handled. It took my breath away to see that much cash in one place, as if somebody had robbed a bank.

For a quarter of an hour I watched him through the window. Then a hound dog that lived on a farm down the road came rambling up on the yard and caught sight of me. I guess he took me for a burglar, because he started to woof. The chief jumped up from the table and came across to the window to look out. I ducked around the corner of the house, the dog at my heels, yammering away.

In another minute, I heard the back door slam, and knew Chief McKenzie was outside. That scared the devil out of me. I took off into some brush. He heard me running and came round the house after me.

"Hey, who is that? What're you doing here?"

There was no stopping me then. I was running flat out, going through hedges, jumping stone walls, kicking at the dog, who was excited by all the action and stayed right up with me, nipping at my shins. I crossed over the main road and went down into a swamp on the other side whose terrain I knew. The dog didn't like that—it was a bog known for snakes—and quit following me after a few minutes. Even then, I didn't stop. I went crashing through pools of muck, up banks covered with ferns, down again into ooze that came over my ankles until I floundered through to the higher ground of the field behind our house.

There, I paused. And listened. Far in back of me, I heard that hound dog baying its head off. I was still in a panic, breathing hard and half expecting Chief McKenzie to come rearing up out of the swamp after me. I ran across the field and crouched down behind our old pump house, where I could keep an eye out in case anyone came across the field to our yard.

Finally the dog quieted down. The night grew peaceful again. My shoes were black with mud. I took them off and sneaked inside, went up to my room and lay down on my bed in my clothes. They were wet, but I didn't care. I was burning up from the run home and couldn't seem to cool down. I lay there sweating, wondering if the chief had recognized me in the dark and, if he had, what he'd do about it.

That night seemed to last forever.

I heard my dad get up, go in the bathroom and head

back to bed. I heard a couple of doves outside my window fluttering their wings and cooing under the eaves where they'd built a nest. Around about 4:00 A.M. the cocks on a farm down near the river began to crow, and still I wasn't asleep. My eyes were wide open. I was out there looking through the McKenzies' window, into that kitchen where I'd eaten so many meals. Jeddy was upstairs asleep in his room, his baseball cap hung on the back of the door. Marina was across the hall in her own bed, dreaming whatever mysterious things girls dream. There were probably ten perfectly legal reasons why Police Chief Ralph McKenzie would be up late counting out stacks of money at his supper table. I just couldn't right then think of what they might be.

HOME IMPROVEMENTS

A WEEK LATER, SCHOOL CLOSED AND THE summer began. The days grew hot, the beaches filled up with rich city folk who had summer houses along the coast.

I began working full-time at the store. Jeddy kept on at Fancher's chicken farm, though I know for a fact he was only part-time because I'd watch him go into the police station across from Weedie's some mornings. He was starting a sort of unofficial apprenticeship, following in his father's footsteps just as he'd told me he planned to. Some mornings I'd hang around outside Riley's to catch his eye as he walked by.

"Hi, Jeddy," I'd say.

"How's it going?" he'd ask me back. That was it. If I tried for anything more, he'd pick up his pace and scoot away. I didn't push it. I remembered what Marina said about him having to work things out. It seemed sad to me that he'd be protecting the honor of his dad's position when Chief McKenzie wasn't exactly living up to that honor himself.

I was wary of the man now, afraid he might have seen

me running away that night and have it in for me. He never said a word, but something about his manner, how his eyes brushed over me when he came in the store for his morning newspaper, gave me warning. "Don't get in my way," that look seemed to say. And I didn't. I ducked back behind the shelves, kept out of his sight. I didn't tell anyone what I'd seen him doing in his kitchen. It wasn't my business, I decided, and anyway, my nose wasn't so clean in that department, either.

From continued espionage on the back stairs, I began to be aware that my own father was dealing regularly, both face-to-face and on the telephone, with racketeers from the Boston gang, under orders from Mr. Riley. The secret room beneath the storage building out back was in constant use. Many mornings, I saw fresh tire marks running across the back lot. Anyone could have noticed. They were heavy marks, the kind a laden truck might leave.

One afternoon, John Appleby slid past me. "Hey, Rube. You want a job tonight?" he whispered.

"What job?"

"There's a boat coming in up at Fogland Point. They're paying twenty bucks a head to unload her."

It surprised me that he'd be involved. He was a year behind me at school and still had the baby face of a ten-year-old.

Thanks but no thanks, I told him. I figured one thing my dad didn't need on top of all his own trouble was me getting caught down on some beach.

"Too bad," John said. "It's going to be fun. A bunch of

us are going down. I guess your stomach couldn't handle it."

"My stomach doesn't have anything to do with it."

"That's right, it's your dad, isn't it? He has you on a short leash, keeping you penned up and pretty for better things."

"Who says?"

"Everybody."

"Like who?"

"Jeddy McKenzie," he said, smirking.

I didn't believe him.

"Jeddy would never say that," I told him, and walked off. John and I had never seen eye to eye. I was given better jobs at the store and had a higher position since I'd been there longer. My impression was he thought I didn't amount to much and had only been hired because of my father.

John Appleby wasn't the only person to offer me shore work that summer. I could've been out a couple of evenings a week if I'd wanted. I began to hear about boys even younger than John who were making twenty or thirty bucks a job. Sometimes their folks would be in on it with them, sometimes they wouldn't be. Even when they weren't, it was obvious they knew what was going on. Parents were closing their eyes to it because the money was so good. You could hardly blame them; many in our town were in low-paying work like farming or fishing and that kind of money was helping them get through.

"It's like picking dollars off a tree," I heard a lobsterman say in the store. "Whether you like it or not, money's growing up there. If you don't put your hand out, somebody else will."

As July turned to August and August crept toward September, the rum-running traffic on our shores went into high gear. At night, I'd hear the hum of tires going over the road accompanied by the barely detectable drone of a muffled engine. Dark vessels slipped along the coast making for beaches that exploded with light and action for a few hours, then went back to being abandoned coves in the morning.

The *Black Duck* was in the news. Aunt Grace saw the article in the morning paper.

"Outfoxed the Coast Guard again," she said in a gleeful whisper over breakfast. My mother, off in the kitchen at that moment, had banned the subject from our table. It pained her, she said, to think of such goings-on. What I thought more likely was that it pained my father to hear about something he wished he weren't part of. That morning, as on nearly every other, he'd already left for the store.

"What happened?" I whispered back.

Aunt Grace leaned foward to show me the story. Two nights before, the *Duck* had been spotted by a Coast Guard cutter going up the West Passage. Ordered to halt and be searched, she'd sped off, leading the Guard on yet another merry chase. It ended with the cutter beached on a tidal sandbar along a barren stretch of coast. The eight guardsmen on board had been forced to swim ashore, swallow their pride and flag down help along the road.

"I bet that about killed them," I said.

"It did!" Aunt Grace laughed. "They're mad as hornets. Listen to this." Bending closer, she read in a low voice:

"*Speaking after the incident, Captain Roger Campbell, officer in charge of the beached Coast Guard cutter, told the* Journal, '*The* Black Duck *is a coastal scourge in this area that must be stopped. Our government will not tolerate brazen lawbreaking of this kind. Someday someone is going to open fire on that boat.*' "

"I've heard of that guy Campbell before," I said. "Isn't he the one who fired on Billy Brady's father?"

Aunt Grace wasn't aware of that, though she'd heard the Brady family was in the rum-running business. I didn't tell her about Billy's connection to the *Black Duck*. He'd probably been on board during the chase, maybe even at the wheel. His wicked grin flashed into my mind, and I imagined the enjoyment he must have had leading Captain Roger Campbell and his crew up onto that sandbar.

My mother came in from the kitchen then, and we closed up the newspaper and began a discussion about whether the Chicago Cubs would get in the World Series against the Philadelphia A's that fall. Aunt Grace was a maniac about baseball, a terrible know-it-all who kept up with all the players and could reel off statistics faster than a ticker tape. Nobody in town could outdo her.

"You'll never find a husband at this rate," my mother

would scold. "You want to build up a man's ego, not squash it down under a pile of facts he should know better than you."

"I can't help it if they're all dumb as doornails," Aunt Grace would fire back, just to irritate my mother even more.

As that summer wore on, it seemed that smugglers were everywhere. You couldn't fish down at the harbor in the evenings for fear of running into liquor landings. Families told their children to stay off the beaches at night lest they stumble on men with guns. Meanwhile, all anybody had to do to buy a bottle was head down to a certain fish hut at the town dock at a certain time of day. And this was small potatoes compared to other sales going on.

The rich summer folks were buying their stuff by the caseload, through their own private bootleggers. That summer of 1929, they entertained like never before, serving cocktails and wine, champagne and brandy on the wide front porches of their elegant seaside homes. Late, late into the night, you'd hear wild dance music coming across the fields from the shore. I got a job bartending at a couple of those parties, learned to make whiskey sours and rum tonics, and how to ice a martini glass. It was an easy way to earn a buck. I would've liked to keep at it, but September arrived. The season came to an end. The summer people went back to Providence or Boston or New York. School started again, and in October the stock market crashed. Huge fortunes went down the drain; jobs began drying up. Nobody felt like celebrating anymore.

That didn't stop people from wanting liquor, though. The smuggling went on. Oh, how it went on. As to who in our town was involved, about the only thing that could be said for sure was a lot of folks were suddenly making home improvements.

I wasn't the only one who noticed that a new roof went on the McKenzie house in early November. Or who heard Fanny DeSousa boasting about her fancy electric stove. John Appleby's parents built a whole barn. Other families were quietly affording indoor bathrooms, new porches, secondhand automobiles.

The Harts were right in there with the best of them, I've got to say. We installed heat in our second-floor bedrooms. My mother went to Providence and bought herself a fox-fur stole. She wore it into Riley's store the next day, looking about as silly as a peacock in a chicken house.

"For pity's sake, keep it at home, can't you?" my father shouted at her when he came back that night. She burst into tears and ran upstairs.

I felt sorry for her. She'd always wanted a stole. Now that they had the money to buy it, she couldn't understand why my father was so angry.

I knew why.

"They're paying me to keep my mouth shut. That's how I make my living now, by shutting up," I heard him tell Aunt Grace later that same night.

"Oh, Carl, you mustn't say that. Don't be so hard on yourself."

"I'm not being hard on myself. If I don't say it, who will?"

"What else can you do? Everyone's in the same boat."

"I could stand up and put a stop to it. I could tell them all to go to hell."

"Tell who?" Aunt Grace asked. "Mr. Riley, you mean? He's no more in charge than the King of Siam!"

That was true enough. While Mr. Riley continued to send orders from his prison cell, the Boston College Boys had long ago taken over the reins of his operation, and many others along the coast. Not only courtroom judges were in these gangsters' pockets. Their influence now extended into the offices of a good number of Rhode Island legislators, as my father well knew. Aunt Grace was right. There was no one to appeal to, and even if there had been, who but a lunatic would blow the whistle on a game that was making so much money for everyone, at every level?

The stakes were about to go higher, though. Unbeknownst to my father and all but a few in our town, a larger and more powerful gang of players was already poised on the horizon, ready to strike.

A NEW WIND

THE FIRST I KNEW ABOUT THE NEW YORK mobsters coming into our area was about a week before Thanksgiving. A stranger with a flashy tan fedora cocked over his forehead came in the store and bought a pack of cigarettes. Then he sat on the public bench just down from our front door to smoke them. Anybody who came by, he struck up a conversation.

"Name's Stanley Culp, and that's a fine old cemetery you've got there behind the church," he'd remark.

Or: "You mean there's a police station in this sweet little town? Can't imagine what ever goes wrong here!"

Or: "What, that place there's the post office? Not much bigger than a postage stamp, is it? Haw, haw!"

He'd raise his hat to the pretty farm wives driving in for supplies. "Morning, ma'am, fine-looking boy you've got there. Nice weather we're having. Yes, I'm from New York City, you guessed right."

The reason people were guessing right about his origins was his car, which was a fancy twin-six engine Packard sedan with New York plates. He didn't let on what his business was, but soon enough people began to understand. He was there for the special purpose of making friends.

He gave fifteen dollars to the Bishop's Fund at St. Mary's and an equal amount to the collection plate at the Congregational Church on Sunday morning. He tucked a dime into the pocket of any child who came past his bench, which picked up business at the store's candy counter a good bit.

When Abner Wilcox, whose wife, Marie, had just died after fifty years of marriage, wobbled up on his cane, Stanley Culp bought him a chocolate bar and talked to him for a solid hour. That was an act of unusual kindness. Though everyone in town was suspicious, we all had to admit that Mr. Culp was doing good.

"And asking nothing in return. *So far*," Mildred Cumming whispered when she came in for a soda pop one afternoon. She'd been keeping her eye on him from the police station.

"Charlie's having kittens wondering who he is," she added. "I've never seen him in such a state."

"What's the chief say?" Dr. Washburn asked her. He'd come by for a hunk of store cheese and some pipe tobacco.

"Chief McKenzie's been out of town all week. Far as I know, he doesn't know anything about it."

"Where'd he go?"

"Took Jeddy up hunting to Vermont for the Thanksgiving holiday. Said he needed a break."

"I can believe that," the doctor replied. "From what I hear, he and Charlie've been spending more time going at each other than after these infernal bootleggers."

Relations between Chief McKenzie and his deputy had gone sour over the summer. They rarely covered cases together anymore, and had been seen arguing in public. Charlie's manner, never specially pleasant on even his best days, was now continuously surly, while the chief went about with a new smugness, as if he'd received some promotion that Charlie didn't qualify for. And perhaps he had. I was still keeping a wary eye on the chief, and one thing I'd noticed was that Mr. Culp's Packard wasn't the only vehicle with New York plates showing up regularly in town. More than a few afternoons, there was another car, a racy black sedan, parked in plain view in front of the police station.

About an hour after Mildred left with her soda, Charlie himself came over. He stood outside the store and started a conversation with Mr. Culp that was soon audible all the way back into the stockroom, where John Appleby and I were stacking crates. We went up front to see what was happening.

"As official law-enforcement deputy of the town, I'm ordering you to vacate these premises!" Charlie was yelling when we got there.

"Oh, come along," Mr. Culp said, giving him a friendly grin. "I've been having a grand time meeting these folks." He gestured toward Dr. Washburn and the small crowd of us who'd come out of the store. Fanny DeSousa was there, and Aunt Grace, too, over from the post office. "Can't see no reason to leave now."

"I know why you're here. You can't frighten me!" Charlie bellowed, sounding scared down to his underwear.

"Frighten you?" said Mr. Culp, looking up lazily. He knew who Charlie was the same way he knew everything about our town. A week of sitting on that bench had accomplished a lot more than just us getting to know him. "Why would I want to frighten you? If I was to want anything, it'd be to say this: if you can't beat 'em, join 'em. That's my message to you."

Charlie brayed out a laugh. "So, you think you're going to join up with us? Hah, that's a good one. You can't barge into a town like this."

Mr. Culp smiled. "No, no, you misunderstand. I'm not doing nothing like barging in. I'm telling you, real nice, it's time to take a powder."

Charlie practically expired with fury over this. "Take a powder! Meaning what?"

Mr. Culp removed his flashy hat and set it down on the bench beside him. "What'd you say your name was?"

"My name is Deputy Sargeant Charles Pope!"

"Yes, Deputy Pope, meaning this. About now, if I was you, I'd be heading on back to that run-down caboose of a police station. I'd put my feet up on the desk and take a good long snooze."

Charlie let out a snort and shook his head.

"Let me put it even more clearly," Mr. Culp went on. "There's a change coming, a new wind in this town. If you try to stop it, why, my guess is it'll blow you down."

All of this was said in a mild tone, as if Mr. Culp was sorry to be speaking these words but saw no way around it. What he meant was only vaguely understood by most of us looking on, but Charlie knew. His eyes bulged and his tongue came out for its snaky flick over his lips.

"You won't get away with this," he snarled. "Chief McKenzie's due back tomorrow. He won't tolerate it!"

Mr. Culp smiled. "Oh, I don't think the chief'll mind too much. Ralph and I have come to an understanding about matters of this kind. Now, go on along before somebody has to take you."

To our amazement, Charlie did. He turned and walked away toward the police station on legs stiff with rage. Stanley Culp watched him. When Charlie had disappeared, he took out his pack of cigarettes and offered them around to the men, passing over John and me and Fanny DeSousa and Aunt Grace. It was still considered improper in our parts for ladies to smoke in public, and like us, they wouldn't have expected to.

"Fine cold weather we're having," Mr. Culp said when he'd seen to it that everybody was lit up. "I hear autumn's the choice season on this coast. Better than spring, they say. Clearer, bluer, beautiful sunrises and sunsets. You never want to leave a place like this in the fall, am I right?"

There was something about the tone of this question that caused us all to nod quickly. Mr. Culp smiled. He put his hat back on, winked at me and launched into one of his New York jokes. It wasn't that funny, but beside me John Appleby gave a big laugh. When I went inside, he stayed to shoot the breeze with Mr. Culp. He was still there a half hour later when my father noticed and ordered him back to work.

The Monday after Thanksgiving, Marina came to find me in an outbuilding behind the store where I was working my afternoon shift.

It was the first I'd seen of her since mid-October. She'd been going out of town that fall, staying with some high school friends in Harveston over the weekends, commuting to school from up there and coming home to catch up on housework during the midweek days. I'd heard she and her father were at odds over it. He wanted her home, taking care of him and Jeddy, the way she had been doing since her mother died. I no longer knew the inside workings of their family, but the word was she'd stood up to him and declared independence. Which she'd won, it appeared. Recently, and not without a lot of grumbling, the chief had started hiring old Mrs. Smithers to come in part-time to cook.

Harveston was where Marina had spent all of the Thanksgiving holiday while Jeddy and the chief were in Vermont. Now they were back and she'd come home, in a blaze of new glamour, I thought. She'd been to Boston and bought a smart wool coat, deep green with a leather collar, high style to my countrified eyes.

She hadn't come by to impress me, though, or to show me any special interest at all. What she wanted was to give me a lecture. Her subject was Mr. Culp.

"Don't you know who he is? He's with the New York mobsters. They're trying to break in around here. You should tell your dad to run him off," she announced, before I'd hardly had time to say hello. That set me on edge.

"My dad said he's sitting on a public bench and it's none of our business," I answered. "Anyway, the guy's giving out cash and people are coming in here and spending it, so we don't mind."

"You should be protecting folks, not setting them up," Marina replied. "The man is looking for a fix, that's plain as day."

"A fix!" I said. "Who does he want to fix?" I'd never heard her talk this way. She seemed to have acquired a whole new vocabulary since we'd last conversed.

"Your dad, for one. He wants him on his side when the shooting starts."

"If there's going to be shooting, why don't you tell your own dad? He's the one with the badge."

I turned to walk off.

"Ruben, wait." Marina caught my arm. "My father won't do anything and neither will yours. They're both in it up to their necks."

"That's a lie!" I told her. "Speak for your own family, not mine." I was offended that she'd lump my father in with hers, when anyone could see there was no comparison.

Marina gave me the kind of glance you give a five-year-old who thinks the moon is made of green cheese.

"There's something else," she said. She lowered her voice. "Remember how those Boston gangsters came in and killed Tom Morrison's dog last spring?"

I glared at her. "Of course I remember."

"They were looking for the ticket to a big liquor shipment."

"I know that, and it's long past," I said. "That shipment must've come in months ago."

"It didn't," Marina whispered. "It's still coming. And the word going around is, the ticket's still good. Over three thousand cases, signed, sealed and paid for. The big syndicates have got wind of it and they're looking to horn in. That's one reason you've got a New York mobster sitting outside your store. Ruben, listen to me: Billy Brady wants to see you."

Suddenly I saw where all this talk of "fixing" and "setting folks up" and "mobsters" was coming from.

"So you're in touch with Billy?"

"We talk now and then."

"That's right, he lives in Harveston." I put two and two together. "Lucky thing you have friends up there."

"Yes, it is. So what?"

From her tone, I suspected there was a lot more going on between her and Billy than she was telling. That galled me. I didn't have a leg to stand on with Marina, but the idea that Billy Brady was moving in on her touched a nerve. All those years eating supper in the McKenzies' kitchen had mounted up in my mind to a form of possession, I guess.

"Billy'll be down at Tom Morrison's late this afternoon," Marina said. "He'll come in by boat. Will you go to see him?"

"I will not! All he wants is to get his own hands on that shipment. He's after money, same as everyone else."

"That's not true," Marina said. "You don't know him. People in Harveston say he's been helping families out from what he makes. That's why his crew's got the good name it has."

"Well, I wish he'd stay away from Tom Morrison," I shot back. "He'll get him in trouble hanging around there all the time. It's not fair to drag an old guy like that into anything to do with the *Black Duck*."

Before I'd even finished saying those words, Marina was reaching to cover my mouth.

"Shh-shh! Not so loud."

I tore her hand off me. "There's nobody around here."

"There's always somebody around everywhere," she whispered. "You just don't notice. And Ruben, they're watching you specially."

"Nobody's paying any attention to me, that's one of my problems." I sent her a furious look.

"They are. It's why Billy wants to see you. There's a new rumor that you've got it. The ticket, I mean, the thing you and Jeddy found."

I'd already guessed that was where this discussion was headed, and it scared me. I wasn't about to show that to Marina, though.

"Who says I have it, Charlie Pope?" I asked, stonewalling the best I could. "Look, I've said it a hundred times, all there was on the guy was his pipe and—"

Marina slapped her hand over my mouth again, and this time I let it stay there. From behind us came a soft squeak. We looked around. The trapdoor in the floor across the room had risen up a little. After a moment of silence, John Appleby came up the ladder out of the old root cellar, a storage area no longer in use since part of it had caved in during the winter.

"John, what're you doing down there?" I demanded.

"Just getting some potatoes," he said. He held up a bag.

"Potatoes are in the side shed now. There's nothing in that place."

"Yes, there is," John Appleby said. "There's potatoes."

He slid by us with a smug look.

"See what I mean?" Marina whispered after he'd gone. "You should be careful what you say."

"John Appleby's not a spy. He's a kid with a big chip on his shoulder is all."

Marina shook her head at me. "Will you go and meet Billy?" she asked again.

"No!" I told her. "Even if I wanted to, I couldn't. My dad won't let me off for anything anymore. We're all working like dogs here to keep up. You tell Billy Brady you

168

delivered the message. Someone is watching me. Well, I'm real glad to hear it!"

I stormed off, and this time Marina let me go. When I looked back, she'd disappeared up front.

I stayed away from that part of the store for the next hour and didn't see her again. Toward the end of the afternoon, though, I opened the trapdoor of the old cellar and looked in. It was black as pitch inside, so I got a book of matches and went down the ladder. All it took was one strike to see that there wasn't a single bag of potatoes in the whole place.

BLACK DUCK SURVIVOR CHARGES COAST GUARD GAVE NO WARNING BEFORE OPENING FIRE

"IT WAS A SETUP," NAVIGATOR SAYS

NEWPORT, JAN. 1—The Coast Guard cutter that intercepted the Black Duck in fog early last Sunday morning gave no warning before unleashing deadly machine gun fire, according to Richard Delucca, the Duck's navigator and sole survivor. Delucca's three shipmates were killed in the barrage, the most violent incident to date along these shores.

"There was dense fog out there and we came up on the cutter so quick that we thought we'd run into it," said Delucca, 24, speaking to reporters for the first time from his bed at Newport Hospital.

"We didn't know it was a government vessel. They gave us no warning shot and no signal to stop. They started firing that machine gun and kept firing. I believe it was a setup. Somebody tipped them off that we'd be coming. Everybody knew Campbell was out to get the Black Duck," Delucca said, referring to Officer Roger Campbell, skipper of C.G. Patrol Boat 290, who gave the order to shoot.

Delucca lost his thumb in the incident. He has been charged with smuggling illegal liquor.

His account was denied by a Coast Guard spokesman. "They were trying to escape. These unfortunate killings resulted from an honest effort to enforce the law," he said.

The Interview

YOU STILL HAD THAT FIFTY-DOLLAR BILL, didn't you? David Peterson asks when Ruben Hart lumbers back from the kitchen, carrying two glasses of lemonade. Outside, a summer rain is cascading down on the yard. They've taken shelter in the dark parlor. The room is hot, even with the windows open.

Don't expect much. It's store-bought, Mr. Hart says, handing over the lemonade. *If my wife were here, we'd be having the real thing.*

That's okay, David says. *I like store-bought.* The truth is, he's never had any other kind.

Did you still have that tobacco pouch under your mattress? David asks again.

Of course.

With the half a fifty rolled up inside?

Would you throw something like that away?

No. One thing I don't understand. Why did Tony Mordello's freighter take so long to show up? Was it lost at sea or something?

For six months? No.

So?

It was always scheduled for a December delivery. That's how Tony Mordello had set it up. He wanted his shipment in time for the holiday season, when he knew he could sell it at a good price. He was buying low and selling high, good business practice.

And then he was shot with the ticket on him, David says.

Hidden in his tobacco pouch, that's right.

How does that work, using a torn bill as a ticket? I still don't get it.

Easy. The captain of the freighter Tony hired to bring his liquor down here has the other half. They did the deal face-to-face up in Canada. Then, when Tony's runners go out to get the shipment in their speedboats, they have Tony's bill and match it with the captain's. Everybody knows they're dealing with the right outfit.

Pretty cool, David says. *It's like a signed contract.*

Mr. Hart smiles grimly. *It's better. There are no names written down, and bills can be folded small. They stand up longer, too—in seawater, for instance. Tony Mordello ran a smart operation. If the College Boys hadn't murdered him, he'd have made a second fortune off the huge cargo coming in on this freighter. His wife could've bought herself another diamond necklace and Cadillacs for the kids.*

So now the Boston College Boys were after you?

Not only them. The New York mob, too. At least, that's what Billy Brady had sent Marina to tell me. I didn't believe him, though, knucklehead that I was.

But how would they have known you even had that fifty?
You'd kept it secret all that time.

One person knew.

Who?

Mr. Hart gets up painfully from his chair. Wet weather raises havoc with his joints.

Let me show you something. He shuffles over to one of the formal, white-doilied parlor tables and fumbles around amid the framed photographs, bending low, trying to find the right one in the parlor's gloom. Whatever pruning Mr. Hart has managed so far with his medieval clippers hasn't improved visibility in here. David, who's had more gardening experience via Peterson's Landscaping than he likes to admit, offered to lend a hand but was turned down. *Help* is a not a word in the old man's dictionary.

Finally Mr. Hart selects a small photo in a silver frame and walks back across the room. He holds it out to David: a black-and-white snapshot of a skinny kid wearing a baseball cap and standing beside a bicycle.

Who do you think that is?

I don't know.

Guess.

Jeddy McKenzie? David says.

You're right. Mr. Hart nods solemnly. *My old friend Jeddy. He'd seen me with the bill in front of my locker.*

But . . . did he tell?

I believe he did. He told the chief.

How could he? He was setting you up.

He was. In the name of police business, that's what he was doing.

He must've thought his dad would step in, somehow. He wouldn't have done it on purpose, would he?

That's a good question. I don't know the answer. Maybe I don't want to know.

THE MUFFLED ENGINE

I WAS IN A BLACK MOOD WHEN I LEFT THE store that afternoon, angry at Marina and sore from unloading stock all day. If I'd been smart, I would have headed straight back to my house and stayed put. But my mother was there, as she always was, ready and waiting to ask how my day had gone.

"Going home, kid?" Stanley Culp gave me the eye as I slouched by.

"Why would I want to go there?"

"So, you're off for a ride? Well, take care of yourself."

I wheeled my bike into the street and pedaled away, feeling his shrewd gaze on my back.

If there was, as there was later said to be, an old Ford station wagon with Massachusetts plates keeping watch on the store from an alley across the road, I paid no attention.

I didn't care, either, that Charlie Pope, hustling away from the police station on some errand, shot me a cool glance over his shoulder and picked up speed.

Chief McKenzie, standing in the station door, was either just coming in or about to leave. His heavy profile faded back out of sight as I passed. Perhaps he was making a note of the direction I was taking, perhaps not. I couldn't be bothered to pick up on such details.

I remember that Ann Kempton, the local seamstress, waved at me from her backyard as she took in laundry from the line.

A group of younger boys was in the field beyond the school whacking a baseball around and whooping it up. They'd been in the store buying sodas earlier, where they'd been warned to keep their voices down and wait their turn at the counter. I knew every one of them by name, such is the closeness of a small town, and now, hearing the crack of the ball on the bat, and their shouts, a darker feeling swept over me.

I was trapped in this place. While Marina visited Harveston and Boston, meeting up with the world, I hauled pickle barrels in Riley's back room, where not even my father looked in on me anymore. He'd given up trying to make me into something he could like.

I laughed cynically, a Stanley Culp kind of laugh. I'd take a ride, all right. I'd go missing for a while. Supper could wait on me for once. Let them wonder where I was.

And so I set out toward the back country, down a road I'd seldom biked which wound away from the sea, past rocky farmland and shrub-clogged forests. The November daylight began to fade and still I went on, furiously at times, suddenly in a rage that even one-eyed Tom Morrison was no longer specially mine. He was Billy

Brady's friend, and Billy's father's before that. The free life he led came out of weakness and retreat, not anything strong he could pass on to me. He was as likely as anyone to bend before the wind.

And what a wind. I imagined Billy now, coming in by boat to the beach, striding up the path to Tom's shack. Billy Brady, tall and broad-shouldered, his white Labrador loping at his side; Billy, with all the glory of the *Black Duck* blazing out, and his easy, joking manner that charmed everyone.

Deep in these thoughts, I rode on through the darkening landscape. Over an hour passed before I thought of going back. My legs had begun to ache. The sun was down by then, and the road dim. An eerie silence rose on all sides and I was suddenly aware that I was far, far out in the country. I was turning to head home when the sound of tires came from the bend ahead. I flicked on my bicycle lamp and drew to the side.

The vehicle, driving without headlights, rode toward me with a ghostly quiet. As it passed, I recognized the whir of a muffled engine and glanced back over my shoulder. It was a Ford coupe, one taillight out.

The vehicle braked, stopped and began to reverse direction. A moment later the car came up in back of me and I squeezed over a second time to let it by. But it hung back and, little by little, moved up closer until I felt the heat of the motor on my legs.

"Come ahead!" I yelled, gesturing for the driver to go

past. He would not. When I looked back to see what the trouble was, a face pushed up close to the windshield and broke into a toothy grin.

Fear spiked through me. Even so, I couldn't believe that anyone could mean me harm. A game is what I thought, and for another hundred yards, I played my part by riding as far to the left-hand side as possible without going in the woods. Finally, with a roar, the big roadster pulled out to pass and I thought I'd be left in peace. But that was not to be. With stealthy calm, the vehicle moved up until the broad side windows were abreast of me. Out of the corner of one eye, I saw faces through the glass.

"Hey! Give me some room!" I called out.

There was no response, and in the next second I saw that I wasn't to be allowed even my slim edge of road. The side of the car moved closer until, with a last impatient swerve, it struck me. I lost my balance and went flying into the woods, where a darkness darker than night dropped over me.

WHERE'S THE TICKET?

THE SOUND OF VOICES DRIFTED DOWN TO me, as if through the depths of an ocean. For a while I was too far sunk to pay attention. Then, slowly, I surfaced and opened my eyes. My head felt heavy and swollen. Without even looking, I knew I was a prisoner.

The room I lay in was cold and dark, with the dank air of a cellar. Faint fingers of light crept in beneath a closed door. I tried to get up and could not. I was bound to a bed of some kind, roped down so tight the twine cut into my shins and wrists.

The voices came from above, along with other noises: chairs scraping, china clinking, the heavy tread of boots. A smell of frying meat and wood smoke wafted down. I guessed that I was lying below a kitchen and that a meal was under way. As I listened, the conversation began to piece itself together.

A man with a flat Boston twang spoke loudest and most often. He was angry about some job that had gone wrong. Cases had been lost, "scuttled" was his word. With that, I knew I was in the hands of a gang of rum-runners.

"Well, we know where we dropped 'em. They're not going anywhere," a younger voice replied.

"So why didn't you go back already?" the Boston voice said. "There's a hundred cases of Johnny Walker Red just lying out there in the harbor? Wait'll the big boys hear that!"

"How're we supposed to get 'em when it's blowing from the north?" a high, nervous voice asked. "You can't do nothing when it's blowing that way."

"The big boys don't care if it's blowing from Timbuktu! You get out tomorrow night and pull up those cases before they wash ashore. Get that guy with the fancy hook that did it for us last time. What's his name?"

"Louie," somebody said.

"Yeah, him. What'sa matter with you guys? You should'a thought of that yourself."

Everybody was quiet for a while. Then someone with a country drawl launched into a story about a new transport van he had that was painted to look exactly like a Bushway's Ice Cream truck. He was laughing about it.

"The Feds are out of the loop on this one! I've got that truck backed up to my cow barn a couple'a times a week, taking on loads for Boston, Providence, wherever. Only thing is, my neighbors next door had been watching. Last week one of 'em buttonholes me and says with a wink: 'All this Bushway's coming and going! You sure must be making a pile of money in the ice cream business.'

"I told him: 'Yeah, we got great ice cream. Comes straight from the isle of Bermuda. You ever try that flavor?'

" 'And what flavor is that?' he asks.

"I say to him: 'Hot buttered rum!' "

A heavy round of guffawing came down through the floor. Then chairs squeaked and it seemed as if the atmosphere changed. A more serious topic arose, one that must have been under discussion before I woke up, because it sort of started in the middle. I took a while to catch the drift, but when I did, my ears were burning.

"How many cases are we talking about?" a voice asked.

"Over three thousand, fancy stuff like champagne and high-priced scotch." This was the Boston accent again.

"Jeez, that's worth a bundle."

"It was scheduled to come in for Christmas. Now the big boys have got word it should be arriving just before New Year's. She's a freighter name of *Firefly*."

"She's coming from St. Pierre?"

"Canada, yeah. Packed to the gills. A private trader. She's bypassing Boston and coming straight down."

"How come?"

"Don't know. Our gang didn't set it up."

"So who did?"

"That big operator who was running around us, Tony Mordello, in New Bedford. He knew he'd make out big on it. Guess what he used for a ticket?"

"What?"

"A fifty-dollar bill ripped in half."

"Fifty bucks!"

"He had it on him when we bumped him off, but nobody knew. Then, one of his boys talked."

"So, who talked?"

"That stoolie cop Charlie Pope. He was in with Tony until he saw what happened to him. Then he decides to come over to our gang to keep the deal afloat since it's already paid for. He stays in touch with the Canadians, pretends Tony's still alive and in charge. Everything's on schedule except no one can find Tony's ticket. Charlie has his suspicions about where it went, but he can't prove it. Then the big boys get a new tip. That's why the kid's downstairs. They heard he's got the ticket stashed away somewhere."

"Where'd the tip come from?"

"Who else? The badge."

"That cop is in on everything."

"Slippery as an eel. I keep warning the big boys, don't trust him. Whoever pays him the most, he goes with. Anyway, if this kid knows where the fifty is, I'm supposed to get it outta him. Hey, Ernie, did you check on the punk lately?"

A minute later, footsteps sounded on the stairs coming down to my cellar. I took a couple of deep breaths, then a key turned in the lock and the door swung open.

My first idea was to keep my eyes shut and play dead. My head was burning up, though, and the ropes were cutting into me. When Ernie looked in, I looked back at him and asked for a drink of water.

"Harry!" he called. "He came to. What d'ya want me to do?"

"Let him alone. I'll be down."

"He's asking for water," Ernie called. "He can't have it till he talks, right?" He was a big man with a wide, fleshy face. Some greasy scrap from supper still hung on his chin.

"Get him some," came the reply.

The door closed. Ernie went back upstairs and returned with a mug, which he tipped so hard into my mouth that most of the water ran down my face.

"Here! Get your head up!" he said. Since even my neck was tied down, this was impossible. Ernie thought that was hilarious. He sat back and laughed at me.

A thin, narrow-eyed man wearing a fisherman's cap stepped into the room. I recognized him right off. Suddenly I knew who Ernie was, too. They were the gangsters with the machine guns who'd shot Tom Morrison's Viola. My blood went cold.

"Let the kid up," the thin guy said. "Nobody can drink lying down."

"Sure thing, Harry."

I was untied and allowed to sit up on the edge of the bed to drink more water. Three other gang members came down to watch. One of them was John Appleby.

"Hello, Ruben," he said, with a sneer.

If I could, I would have spit in his face. I'd figured out by then that this was the Boston gang headed up by the College Boys. Marina was right, they'd been all around me, watching and waiting. I'd been a blind fool.

As soon as I'd drunk my fill, Harry started in on me. He was the one with the Boston drawl.

"We know you picked that body on the beach. We

know *what* you picked, too, so don't bother with the funny stuff. Where's that fifty-dollar bill?"

"What bill?" I said.

"You know what. Your little friend saw it." Harry stabbed his finger into my chest. "He says you put it in a schoolbook. Where is it now?"

I kind of choked. I'd more or less forgotten Jeddy had seen me drop the bill in front of our lockers. Even worse, though, I couldn't believe he'd tell on me. My mouth got dry.

Harry moved in so his breath was on my face.

"What's your name, kid?" he asked.

From behind him, John Appleby answered for me. "Ruben Hart. His dad is manager of Riley's store."

"Now, Ruben, listen up. We don't want to hurt you. We want to get you back to your dad as soon as possible. This is just business, see? That bill is part of a deal we're doing. We've got to have it or the deal won't go through. So, where's this book? At school?"

If only that bill still was in my book at school, I would've told them. If I'd had it on me, I would've handed it over in a minute. What did I care about some freighter from Canada? The trouble was, it was in the tobacco pouch under my mattress at home, and I didn't want Harry or Ernie or any of those gangsters going anywhere near my house. My mother and Aunt Grace were there, probably by themselves.

"I don't have it anymore," I told Harry.

"C'mon, kid. We're not stupid."

"I threw it away."

"That's a good one."

"I did. How did I know anybody'd want it? You can't buy anything with half a fifty dollar bill. I kept it for a while, then I threw it away."

"Where? When?"

"At school, in the wastebasket in my classroom, about a week ago."

Harry's eyes went narrow. I could see he didn't believe me and was trying to make up his mind what to do about it. The rest of the gang stood around like vultures, watching.

"C'mon, boss, let me pop him a few times," Ernie said. "He'll talk."

Harry looked as if he was considering this when a phone started ringing upstairs.

"Get that," he ordered. John Appleby went for it. You could see he was low man on the totem pole, the same as he was at the store. After a minute, he yelled down:

"Harry! It's the badge."

"That weasel. What does he want?"

"He says to quit working on the kid. On orders from the big boys."

"What? Why?"

"The badge says he got a call from Boston. There's been a change of plans. They're sending somebody else over to talk to the kid."

Harry went into a string of terrible curses when he heard this. "Here I've done the dirty work and caught the punk, and now they're turning him over to somebody else? That doesn't make sense. Hold the phone, I'm coming up."

"He hung up already."

A grim look came over Harry's face when he heard this.

"I smell a rat. I'm calling Boston to check this. You take over with the kid," he told Ernie, and went off.

I was petrified. I knew if I was left in Ernie's hands, I'd be dead, or knocked out again at the least. Just looking at Ernie told you he lived his life on a short fuse. Any little thing could set him off. He'd shot Viola for tripping over her.

Harry must have had second thoughts, too, because halfway up the stairs he stopped and yelled back.

"Wait! Tie the kid up again. And Ernie, don't touch him. You hear me? I don't want no mark on him when I come back."

So I was tied down to the bed again. Ernie looked disappointed not to be able to work on me, but he followed orders. Since I was awake, he gagged me this time. When he finished, John Appleby, who'd been hanging around smirking, gave my bed a kick.

"How d'ya like that?" he said. "You're in trouble now and your daddy ain't here to fix it, is he?"

I tried to look daggers back at him, but he just laughed at me. Then he and Ernie closed me in and went upstairs. I was alone in the dark again, except for those little fingers of light coming under the door. I began to get scared.

For one thing, I was wondering who this cop "the badge" might be. Or rather, I wasn't wondering, I was pretty sure I knew. The air around me suddenly got colder and denser. The walls of the cellar seemed to creep in on me. I tried to wiggle my feet and hands to keep the blood flowing, but slowly the feeling went out of them. I gave up and lay still. Whatever was ahead for me, I knew I didn't have anything but a prayer to raise against it.

SEEING STARS

TIME PASSED, I COULDN'T TELL HOW MUCH. Hours, maybe. I dozed on and off. At one point, I heard a knock on the door upstairs and a lot of feet stamping around overhead. There was some talking. I couldn't make out the words.

I heard the next thing all right: a gun went off from a place that seemed right over my bed. My heart took a giant leap. Upstairs in the kitchen, someone swore and another shot let loose. I heard a body fall down, then a bunch of grunts and crashing furniture. A fight was going on. A few minutes later, it stopped, and footsteps came thudding down the stairs to my cellar. The door blasted open. A couple of brand-new characters walked in.

"Found him!" one yelled. He came over and started trying to yank me off the bed.

"He's tied down," the other guy said.

"Well, cut him loose."

The second man flicked open a jackknife and cut me free. They both started trying to drag me up the stairs.

"C'mon, kid. Walk!" they were telling me, but my legs had gone dead. I couldn't make them work. Finally, one of them hauled me over his shoulder like a sack of flour and we went up.

"Where am I going?" I asked.

"Shut up," he said.

We came to the top of the stairs and turned down a hall that led to the front door. On the way, I saw Harry and Ernie standing in the kitchen with their hands in the air. Somebody was holding a gun on them and they didn't look happy about it. John Appleby had a gun on two others. The little squealer had switched sides.

A man was lying on the floor. Whether he was shot dead or just wounded, I couldn't tell because I was traveling sort of upside down and backward. I caught a glimpse of Harry turning around to watch me as I went by.

"Who are you guys?" I heard him say to one of the boys holding the guns. "Hey, we can cut a deal. You want in on the freighter? Tell the badge we got no problem with that. We didn't know he wanted to go that way. We got no problem at all."

Nobody answered. Harry looked as if he couldn't believe what was happening. I couldn't believe it, either. I was being kidnapped again.

My head slammed into a hard edge. I saw a fountain of sparks and then a warm, wet curtain came down over my eyes. I'd been thrown into the backseat of a big roadster and now a bunch of guys were piling in after me. The engine cranked up and we started away down the road. The man sitting next to me was angry.

"Idiot! He's bleeding like crazy. Why'd you dump him like that?"

"I didn't!"

"Can you stop it?"

"Get that blanket outta the trunk."

My head was feeling strange, woozing in and woozing out. They tried sitting me up, laying me down, wrapping handkerchiefs around my head and covering me up with the blanket. Nothing would stop me. I was bleeding all over the place.

"He's going to need a docter," somebody said. "We can't deliver him this way. Take the gag off."

When they got it off me, another voice in the front seat said: "We ain't got time for no docter. Listen, kid, we didn't mean to hurt you. Can you breathe better now?"

I nodded. There was something familiar about that voice. I'd heard it before.

"Cripes, he's a mess. Farino, what were you thinking, throwing him in like that? You know he's gotta talk!"

"Well, he weighed a ton."

"What'd he hit?"

"A case of booze."

"Cripes!"

The car went very fast at times and slowed down to a crawl at others. There were a number of turns and swerves. They'd laid me down on my back on the seat, my legs stretched across two or three laps. Whenever I opened my eyes, I could see stars shining in the dark sky through the car window. I recognized a couple of constellations

Jeddy and I used to point out to each other: Orion's Belt and Scorpio. I saw the Big Dipper. After a while, we must have been driving in more or less one direction because the same constellations stayed there, inside the window frame. I'd get dizzy and close my eyes, and when I opened them, Orion would still be riding along with me. I didn't know where I was going but even in my bad state, I knew who I was going with. Somewhere along the way, I figured out who that voice in the front seat belonged to.

Stanley Culp.

I was traveling with the New York mobsters.

"Hello, Mr. Culp. It's me, Ruben Hart," I remember saying once. I was dumb enough to think he'd somehow missed this fact.

He glanced at me over a shoulder in his lazy way. "Sorry about this, kid," he said, and turned back around.

I must have passed out because the next thing I knew, I was being carried from the car and taken inside another house. The room I was put in this time was upstairs, a kind of attic. I was still bleeding, going in and out of consciousness. At some point, a man with a face that sagged like a old sack down one side came to look at me. I figured he was one of the kingpins because everyone was kowtowing to him, holding his coat and backing up to give him room. He leaned over and gave me a hard stare.

"Poor kid. You messed him up good," he said.

That was it. He left. He'd decided I was beyond talking at that moment, and he was probably right. The funny thing was, I was ready to talk if only I could have. I was scared sick. These New York gangsters struck me as real efficient professionals, the kind that don't play around with dumping bodies at sea that might wash up on shore later. If they wanted to get rid of someone, they'd know how to do it. Like Danny Walsh in Providence, there'd be nothing left behind and no one to tell why.

Later, when I found out that the man with the sagging face was probably Lucky Luciano himself, come out from New York City for the very purpose of directing operations in our area, I wasn't surprised. A face like that you don't forget. A face like that could've asked me and I would've told him: "Under the mattress, in the tobacco pouch." My mother and Aunt Grace would've had to take their chances.

After a few hours, one of the New York gang brought me up a bowl of soup and stood around while I tried to eat it.

"If I were you, I'd get better fast and talk," the guy said. He had a sort of deadpan face. There was no telling what he was thinking.

"I will," I croaked.

"They don't want you around here. They'll get rid of you."

"Thanks," I said.

"Even if you talk, they'll probably get rid of you," he went on. "It's cleaner that way. Nobody to squeal on us."

After that, I couldn't eat anymore. He took the soup bowl, tied me up and put the gag over my mouth. He turned out the lights on me the way the Boston gang had done, closed the door and went downstairs. The only window in the room had a shade pulled over it. I was alone in the dark, and this time there were no fingers of light to hang on to. I began to drift.

At times I seemed to be on a rolling sea, and at other times I lay in a dark forest, trees waving over my head. I imagined myself floating up toward a ceiling, which I expected to bump into at any moment, though I never did because it always lifted higher in the nick of time to make room for me. What I found out was, there's a point beyond which you can't bring up enough energy even to be afraid anymore. What was happening was happening, and I wasn't me but a spectator to myself, waiting and watching and, in an oddly distant way, curious to see how it would end.

Sometime later, a loud creak woke me up. I thought a piece of roof was being pried off right over my head. I waited but nothing else happened. I'd decided I'd been imagining things again when a quieter sound started, a sort of gnawing or jimmying. It came from the window in my room. I heard whispering. Someone was trying to get in.

Suddenly, the window was raised. A wave of cold air blew in from outside. The shade buckled and was pushed aside, and a leg came in over the sill. Somebody was in the room with me. A black shape stood just inside the window, looking around, trying to get its bearings. I held my breath. After everything that had happened, I didn't know if it was a friend or someone else out to get me.

At last, a voice whispered: "Ruben? Are you in here?"

"Mm-mm-mm," I said through my gag.

The dark shape came forward and stooped over me. A cigarette lighter came on in my face. In its flash, I saw Billy Brady, and he saw me.

"Gotcha!" he whispered, and squeezed my arm. "Here, hang on to to this."

He put the burning lighter into one of my hands that was tied to the bedpost, then set to work with a knife to cut through my ropes. One by one, he sliced them off. He pulled me up and unknotted the gag over my mouth. I was never so happy to see anyone in my life.

"How did you know I was here?" I said. I was groggy, still not sure if this was a dream or real life.

"Shh-shh!" Billy leaned close and said in my ear: "Don't talk now. There's a ladder set up outside the window. I'll be right behind you. Move real slow."

Slow was the only way I could move after being tied up for so long. I inched across the room, climbed out the window and went down that ladder one shivery leg at a time. It seemed an age before my foot hit the ground. Then Billy came down beside me and, hardly breathing, we went across the dark yard to the road. We were almost there when someone rushed at me from behind a bush and two arms went around my neck. A voice said, "Thank God!" in my ear.

I didn't have to look to know who it was. Marina McKenzie. When she'd finished hugging me, she started up shaking me.

"Next time listen when someone tells you to watch out," she hissed. "You could've ended up dead."

"I know," I whispered. "I think John Appleby set me up. He was playing both sides."

"That skunk. No wonder his family was getting rich. Anyhow, we've got you back, so it's all right."

There was no more time to talk. We began sneaking away down the road behind the tall, dark form of Billy Brady. He wasn't alone. Two men came up behind us carrying the ladder. Around the bend, two cars were waiting, idling with their headlights off.

Billy went over and talked to the driver of one and sent him off on some errand. Then we all piled into the other car, an old station wagon. Marina, Billy and I were in the backseat while the others sat up front with the driver.

"No talking till we get past these crooks," Billy warned. The driver nudged the accelerator and started off coasting to keep the engine quiet. We drifted past the house where the New York mobsters had held me. Not a sign of movement came from inside.

"Out cold from celebrating too hard, most likely," one of Billy's friends snickered after a minute.

"Those New York goons thought they'd pulled a double whammy on the College Boys," a second one said. "Ruben here wasn't the only thing they hijacked. While the one bunch was holding everybody at gunpoint in the kitchen, the rest of the gang was out back with a truck, helping themselves to a shedful of the College Boys' whiskey. Must be a hundred cases they brought back with them, stacked behind the house."

"There *was* a hundred cases, you mean," the first man said. "Rick, tell Billy what we did."

"Alfred and I laid claim to a few while you were springing Ruben. We've got 'em in the back with the ladder."

They all let loose and whooped at that.

"You fellas've got the stickiest rum-running fingers I ever saw!" Billy said. Turning to me, he added, "I hope you don't mind a bunch of renegade smugglers being your angels of mercy."

I grinned and said it was all right by me.

"Then I'd like to introduce you to the crew of the *Black Duck*. It's thanks to them we could pull off this stunt."

As the car picked up speed, hands started coming out to me in the dark, and though I couldn't see their faces very well, I tried to thank each one for coming to my rescue. There was Alfred Biggs, ship's mechanic, with forearms the size of tree stumps. There was Rick Delucca, Billy's partner and navigator on the *Duck*, who'd known Billy at Harveston High School and brought him in on the *Black Duck*'s operations after Billy's dad was killed. Behind the wheel was Bernardo Rosario, the *Black Duck*'s radio man, even younger than Billy, though he had a wife and two kids at home.

"How did you find me?" I asked him. "I thought I was a goner."

"You never were, Marina had you under surveillance,"

Billy answered. "In case you don't know, she's our trusty watchdog on land," he added, no doubt thinking he was paying her a compliment, much as he prized his friendship with those animals.

"Trusty watchdog!" she protested. "I certainly hope not!"

"Secret agent, then, or how about Director of Intelligence? We had a notion you were about to get snatched by those Boston foxes, Ruben, and were keeping an eye out. We would've rescued you quicker, except the New York gang beat us to it. I hadn't figured on them. We were trailing you all over."

I looked at Marina then, wondering if she had any idea of the part her father had played in my abduction. I suspected she didn't, and kept quiet on that subject. The truth is, I wasn't sure about the chief myself. He was into the racket so deep, on so many levels, it was impossible to guess what his game plan was. I could bet my safety wasn't high on his scoreboard, though.

"So, you're working for the *Black Duck* now?" I asked Marina. I knew she had a mind of her own, but that was the first I'd had an inkling she'd take it so far.

"Not at all," she said. "I'm trying to keep them out of trouble."

Everybody roared with laughter at that. ("Fat chance," Alfred Biggs told her.) I was glad we'd gone a piece down the road or the New York gang might have been woken up and come after us. The *Black Duck*'s crew was a cheerful, wisecracking bunch. As for Captain Billy Brady, whatever I'd thought of him before, I changed my mind that night. I knew he'd risked his skin for me, and asked his friends to do the same. There'd never be a way I could properly thank him, even if his motives weren't completely pure. Which they weren't, as I found out a moment later.

"Now, Ruben," Billy said, leaning toward me in the car. "Where is this ticket you've got? The word going around is it's half a fifty-dollar bill, ready to match with the captain of the *Firefly*'s. You know that boat's carrying over half a million dollars' worth of goods."

I was opening my mouth to announce exactly where it was, thinking it was the least I could do for him, when I felt a hand take mine under cover of dark.

"Ruben threw it out, didn't you?" Marina said softly, looking straight ahead.

I didn't know what was going on, so I kept quiet.

"You wouldn't toss it!" Billy said. "Come on, Ruben, you didn't do that."

"He did. He told me," Marina went on, keeping my hand deep in hers. "About a month ago, wasn't it?"

"Yes," I said.

"He didn't know what it was," Marina went on.

I nodded. "That's what I told the Boston gang, too. What good's half a fifty-dollar bill?"

"Wait a minute!" Billy yelled at Marina. "If you knew he'd tossed it, why didn't you say so? You could've let me know before we went to all this trouble to snatch him."

She locked eyes on him with that level gaze of hers.

"Billy Brady, I'm astonished. What were you intending to rescue, Ruben or the ticket?"

Billy sagged back against the seat, shaking his head.

"That beats all," he groaned. "The *Firefly*'s finally coming in after all these months and now there's no one to claim her cargo. Her captain will see there's been a misfire and probably turn tail and head to Canada. Tony Mordello would have a good laugh over that. All his liquor going back out to sea. I guess he won the last round at that poker game after all."

"I guess he did," Marina answered, giving me a knowing smile. She squeezed my hand and let it go.

I never asked Marina why she made me tell that lie, but it wasn't hard to figure out. Anyone could see that the *Firefly*'s shipment was too big and too hot for a small smuggling operation like the *Black Duck*'s. Billy Brady's interest in profit had begun to get the better of his good sense. Marina was doing exactly what she'd said, trying to keep the *Duck* out of trouble, though even then she must have known she was playing against the odds.

All the time we were driving the dark roads back to town, I'd assumed I was headed home. Not until the car took a sharp turn and began to bump over a surface that was obviously not the road into my house did I look out. There, just visible in the faint light of what was now early dawn, I saw a span of choppy ocean that could only be the water off Coulter's Point.

"Aren't you taking me home?"

The car went silent.

"Not right away," Billy said after a pause. "Your name's out and around about this ticket. We think it's best if you lay over with a friend of the family until things settle down. Your parents know you're safe. I sent word by Doc Washburn in the car back there."

"Doc Washburn! Was he in on this?"

"He was. The doc knows this town inside out. He's no rumrunner, but we call on him if we need him. Your father's been worried sick about you. I've been in touch about tonight. Our plan was, if we got you back, you'd be safer away from home. He said he'd spread a story you've gone to visit your brother in Providence. That should cover you for now."

I tried to imagine my father being worried sick about me, but couldn't bring up that picture. More likely, he'd be worrying about who he'd find on such short notice to do my work at the store.

At this point, the car slowed and rocked even more crazily over the ground, and a dog started barking.

"Sadie! Stop that racket!" Billy shouted out the window.

A second later, we came up on two chicken coops leaning together at an angle that looked as if a hurricane had been through. I knew what friend of the family he'd been talking about.

A SAFE HAVEN

TOM MORRISON WAS EXPECTING US. A LARGE oil lantern was hanging on a hook outside his door, casting a faint light across the cluttered yard. I was dead tired by this time. My head had started bleeding again and I had a hard time of it just to walk inside. I remember Marina sitting me down at Tom's table and offering me a steaming cup of her very own clam chowder. She'd made up a batch at home and brought it to leave with Tom so I'd have something she knew I liked to eat. But that morning I could hardly stay upright in the chair.

"Leave him be for now," I heard Tom say. "He's gone through the grinder. You and Billy go along. I'll look after him, don't you worry."

The next thing I knew, the room was empty, and Tom was taking off the towels that were wrapped around my head. He bathed my wound in warm water, and wrapped it again in some kind of cloth. Sadie tried to lay her head in my lap, but Tom told her to keep off me. I believe I finally ate a little, and drank a quantity of water before sleep took me out on a great dark tide. Not until evening did I open my eyes and find myself in Tom's bunk. And there he was a minute later, looking down on me as gentle as a nurse.

"Looks like the three of us is going to be shipmates for a spell," he said.

He was including Sadie in his count, and well he might. She was right there leaning over me with him, only lower down, drooling sympathetically on my face.

I pushed her snout away. "Is Sadie living with you now?"

"She's consented to have me for the time being," Tom replied, ruffling her ears so her feelings wouldn't be hurt at being shoved off. "Billy don't want her on the *Duck* no more. Says it's getting too hot out on the water, what with the shooting and double-crossing going on these days."

"Did she used to do his jobs with him?"

"Oh, Lordy, yes! She's an old smuggling hand. Get Billy to tell you about her sometime. She can smell a Coast Guard cutter around a bend. Sets up to yipping. Out on West Island, there's a drop she guards. The thieves keep away, knowing she'll tear them to shreds if they so much as put one foot ashore."

"The *Black Duck*'s got a place out on West Island?"

At this, Tom clapped his hand over his mouth. "I'm talking too much," he said. "You just forget what I said. This isn't your business and you don't want to know about it."

For once, I didn't mind that at all. I really didn't want to hear any more about smuggling or rumrunners at that moment. Tom went off to fix me a bowl of Marina's

204

chowder, leaving Sadie and me to start getting to know each other better.

That was the beginning of what I look back on now as one of the happiest times in my life. For the next couple of weeks, I stayed with Tom and he took care of me. I was up and about in a day or so, though I had to be careful not to move too fast or my head would spin. We'd crossed into December by then and the days had a frigid edge to them, though a bright sun seemed always to be beaming down around Tom Morrison's chicken coops. Maybe it was just being out from under my old life, away from the hum-drum of schoolwork and Riley's General Store, but I felt like a bird escaped from a cage.

We spliced rope and wove crab traps on the stoop the first few days. Then, though the season was drawing to a close, I went out crabbing with Tom on his raft. Sadie came, too. He was teaching her to spot crabs underwater, the job Viola'd had.

"One-eyed folks like me don't get a read on depth the way most people do," Tom explained. "The world's kind of flat to us, though you get so's you fill it out with some imagination of your own. The trouble with crabs is, there's no room to imagine 'em if you want to catch 'em. They're either there or they're not. Am I right, Sadie?"

She'd just then come out of the water after a dive off the raft, and her answer was to start shaking herself from head to tail, thoroughly dousing us with freezing pond water. It got so bad, we had to push her back in.

When we weren't on the raft, we skulked around on

the beach, looking for interesting objects that might've washed up. I told Tom about a bride's hope chest Jeddy and I had found one time full of sheets and towels and ladies' silk underthings. We were so embarrassed that we dug a hole and pushed the whole mess in before anyone could catch us with it.

Tom said that was by no means the most unusual thing. A crate of Florida oranges had washed up on his shore once, ripe and delicious. He'd eaten every one.

More darkly, he told me of a boot he found with a human foot still in it.

"Was it the mob, do you think?"

He said it might've been, though this was a few years before their kind of murderous activity was widespread.

"Could've been sharks or ocean currents or any number of things," he went on. "You never know with the sea. It's a place unto itself. There's baby seals who get parked here on this beach by their mothers. They'll be migrating down the coast, usually early in spring, and the little ones grow tired. The pup'll be here a day or two, laying over, then the mother'll come back to pick him up and they'll start off on their travels again.

"Gives you a strange feeling coming across one of those pups. They've got a human child's eyes, but how they look at you, it's unnerving. Like they're in touch with some wildness no human could ever know. They're from an undersea world that's far beyond our knowledge, with rules and reasons that have nothing to do with ours. A privilege it is to live alongside such a mystery, and have the chance once in a while of staring it in the face."

In the evenings, Tom would light his kerosene lantern and cook up some supper. There wasn't ever much doubt what it would be. I had crab in just about every way a crab can be made edible, in soup, grilled, poached, stewed, steamed, fried, baked, fricasseed and then some. Sadie ate right along with us.

After dinner, we'd sit with our feet up on the warm cast-iron stove and talk or not, whatever we felt like. There was no need to be polite or say something you didn't mean just to fill up space in the conversation. Nobody was harping on anyone to wash up or take off his boots. Nobody was watching the clock about when to go to bed. It was heaven to me, and an eye-opener, too, that Tom had found a way to live that was the right way for him, even if it wouldn't agree with what other people might think.

Never once did Tom dig into the reason why I was there, and that was good of him since I didn't want to think about the fool I'd been to get myself kidnapped. My head wound was healing and my heart was, too, I guess, because the darkness that had been in me for weeks, worrying about my father and the store and where I was headed in life, cleared off. I was whistling on my way to the woodpile—it was cold enough so the stove in Tom's shack was going by then—and ruffling Sadie's ears right along with Tom.

December moved on, and Christmas came and went without anyone bothering much about it. Tom had his own take on seasons and holidays that was completely out of time with the rest of the world. Billy's crewman Alfred Biggs came down and brought me a sweater my mother had knitted for me, and a book from Aunt Grace, and that was about all there was to it. No tree or decorations or singing or turkey dinner. What I found out was, they didn't matter to me as much as I'd thought they did. I was happy without. It occurred to me that some of Tom Morrison was beginning to rub off on me.

It wouldn't last, of course. Couldn't last. Out to sea, I'd watch laden schooners tacking upwind, or fishing sloops sneaking into coves beyond Coulter's at dusk. I'd hear a seaplane buzz over the bay and I'd know that real life was out there with its shifting fogs and confusion, ready to come in on me again given the slightest excuse.

One bright, unusually warm afternoon at the end of December, it came. I was down on the beach by myself looking for washed-up fish heads the inshore trawlers might have dumped that would do for a soup. Crabs had begun to disappear with the cold and Tom was moving on to his winter menu. From the direction of West Island, a dark speck appeared on the water. In short order it became a boat heading toward the mainland at a high rate of speed, a white plume of water rising off her stern. Right away, I knew she wasn't headed for the harbor or any other place. She was coming straight in to Coulter's. I took off back to Tom's shack to warn him.

He'd spotted her already and was out front, up on a dune, squinting against the sun. Sadie was standing tense beside him, preparing to bark her head off as usual. As I came up, Tom laid a hand on her snout and said:

"Looks like we got visitors."

"Is it . . . ?" I was afraid to say. All I was thinking about was thugs and machine guns.

"No. Not them." He cupped his hand like a spyglass around his good eye. "I believe it's a craft you don't often catch a glimpse of in the light of day."

A minute later, as we both watched, the speedster roared into Coulter's at full throttle, cut engine and turned sideways to the beach. At the helm, the dark outline of the skipper was visible in his captain's cap, working the controls. Even at that distance, I knew him.

Billy Brady was one of those fellows that stand out a long way off. As the *Black Duck* drifted softly in toward the beach, I saw a girl come up beside him in the wheelhouse, a red bandana tied over her long, brown hair.

"Marina!" Tom exclaimed. "Go meet 'em, Sadie."

He let the dog free and followed her down the path as fast as he could hobble. Last of all, I went, eager to see them, too, but sad as well, guessing this arrival meant my happy days with Tom Morrison were nearing an end.

FOG

THERE WAS JUST BILLY AND MARINA ON board the *Duck* that warm blue day. To see them side by side, dropping anchor, securing the line on deck, lowering the little skiff into the water and, Billy at the oars, rowing in to shore over the waves, was to know without a doubt that they'd thrown in their lot together. They were laughing and fooling around like a couple of kids. Whatever hope I'd had, if you could even call such an impossible dream "hope," that Marina would wait for me to catch up with her in life blew away.

It was no use being jealous or angry at Billy. He was above and beyond anything I could be. They stepped out of the skiff holding hands, grinning over some private joke, barely aware of Tom and me calling out our hellos as we came down the beach.

Then Sadie was on them, wild to see Billy after all that time, galloping around in circles and barking so loud, nobody could hear a word. Billy brought out a ham bone he'd saved up for her, and wrestled her for it. At last she got it away and took off into the dunes.

"You're a nervy pair to be out on the *Duck* in broad daylight!" Tom teased them as we walked down the sandy path to his cabin. To Billy, he said, "I hear the whole United States Coast Guard is out to lay you low."

"Well, I've got nothing on board this afternoon. They'll have to be patient!" Billy kidded back.

"Nothing but Marina McKenzie, the brightest pearl in the sea," old Tom said. He grinned at her. "I hope you know you're putting yourself at risk traveling with this scurrilous pirate."

"I believe I've decided to take that risk," Marina replied. Though she said it with a smile, a darker tone was in her voice. I guessed she was under no illusion as to what she'd entered into.

"Come on in," Tom said when we came to the cabin. "Can I take it for granted that you'll both stay for supper? You'll be surprised, I'm sure, to hear we're having crab. It's the last of it, though. Ruben and I are going on to fish-head chowder tomorrow."

Billy laughed and said it would be a special pleasure to stay, due to the tricky situation they were in.

"And what's that?" Tom asked.

"Marina can't be seen with me in town," Billy answered. "Her dad's laid down the law. He's a great believer in defending a woman's honor."

"He needn't worry. I'm doing that perfectly well by myself," Marina countered, giving Billy a push.

"You are!" He laughed. "I can't make a dent."

Marina turned to me. "Billy's not taking it serious, as

you can see, but it's true about Dad. He heard about us getting together up in Harveston. That snake Charlie Pope found out and told him."

"I thought Charlie and the chief weren't getting along."

"They aren't, which is the very reason Charlie went and told. He was aiming to get back at me and Dad all in one swoop. It's worked, all right. My father's on the warpath against Billy."

"Does he know you're in with the *Duck*?" Tom Morrison asked Billy.

"If he doesn't know by now, he's blind, deaf and dumb," Billy said. "What he can do about it is another question."

This boastfulness didn't go over well with Marina. A worried wrinkle came up on her forehead and she seemed about to speak when Billy announced it was time to get on with things. He told Tom he had a plan to put before him. The two went inside the cabin for a private talk. Marina drew me back outside to give me the latest news of home.

"Everybody's fine. They're holding to their story of you being with your brother, though folks in town are beginning to wonder what's taking you so long up in Providence. The school's on your case, too. Your father told them you're taking classes up there. He said no one would know the difference once you got back. You'd catch up in a blink with all the brains you've got."

"He said that about me?" I swear it was the first compliment I'd ever had from him.

Marina nodded. "He did. He's missing you, Ruben. This whole episode's given him fits."

We sat down on Tom's stoop in the last of the afternoon sun. Out to sea, a strange fog was gathering over the waves. It appeared that the warmth of the day was having an unusual effect, for rarely did the ocean produce mist in winter.

"What's happening with Jeddy?" I asked. I'd been thinking of him a lot.

"You know, he's been wondering the same about you," Marina said. "That's something he'd like to fix."

"What is?"

"The two of you. He said he wants to get back together sometime."

"Well, how about right now? Does he know where I am? Tell him to come down for a visit."

"Oh, Ruben," she said. "If only I could. He thinks you're up in Providence, like everybody else. The way things are, it's probably better he doesn't know the truth."

"But why?" I asked. "He wouldn't tell, would he?"

Marina sighed. "I don't know. There's a lot between us we don't dare talk about."

Jeddy had quit at Fancher's, she said, but was still in and out of the police station, following his father more closely than ever.

"He knows Dad's been a partner on some pretty shady deals, but he'd rather overlook it," she said. "It doesn't fit with Jeddy's view of what he'd like to believe. I'm just as bad if it comes to that. We're both shutting our eyes. In the beginning, Dad just did small favors for favors in return. He'd stay away from certain beaches on certain nights, or keep the State Patrol off roads where liquor was being trucked through. Now I think he's in deep with a big-city gang and doesn't know how to get out."

I thought this a mild description of the chief's activities after what I'd heard and seen during that year, but I kept my mouth shut.

"I wish my mother were here," Marina went on. "She'd set him straight. He never speaks to Jeddy and me about it, of course."

"Of course." I knew how that was. My heart went out to Jeddy. I saw how he was caught in the snarl of the liquor racket even worse than I was. If he stood by his old rule of "police business," he'd have to turn the chief in, and if he stood by his dad, he'd be lying to himself about what he knew was a crime.

Beside me, Marina sighed and shook her head. "Sometimes I stop and wonder what's right," she said. "And there isn't any answer, so I just go along. I guess, in the end, if you have to make a choice, you do what's best for the people you love."

I nodded, though I wondered how Marina herself would ever apply that rule. She had her father on one side and Billy Brady on another, and neither of them were on the right side of the law. I didn't know what I'd do if I were in her shoes, so I didn't say anything. We sat silent together watching that unseasonable fog rolling toward us in great white billows. It was the sort of fog that, once it's settled over the bay, hangs on till morning, giving plenty of cover to anyone who might need it.

"What's Billy got going for tonight?" I asked.

Marina glanced up. "Well, you might as well know since you'll find out soon enough. A boat's come in from Canada with a big load of holiday liquor. It's a shipment that could make up for some of what he might've had if the *Firefly* had come through. The whole crew is going out in the *Black Duck* to bring it ashore. They want to land the cases here at Coulter's, and store them overnight with Tom. If Tom'll allow that. Billy's trying to talk him into it right now."

"So Tom hasn't been in on things?"

"He doesn't like the liquor-smuggling business. It was losing Viola that turned him against it, I think. He's never gotten over the way she was killed."

"You don't go on jobs with Billy, do you?" I asked.

"I have," she admitted. "It's a wild ride, all right. Lately, there've been too many close calls. The Coast Guard's been stepping up their patrols. It's harder than it was to get a speedboat in shore. Also, the big gangs are muscling into Billy's territory. There's always danger some stool pigeon like Charlie Pope will hear about one of his jobs and rat to the Coast Guard."

"So the Coast Guard is taking bribes, too?"

"Some are and some aren't, the same as everywhere. A lot of officers are honest enough, but the *Black Duck* has slipped through their fingers once too often. They wouldn't mind a hot tip on her whereabouts, no matter who it comes from. I wish Billy'd quit, but I know he never will," she added. "The money's too good. He's making ten times what he ever did fishing."

At this point, Tom Morrison gave us a shout from inside. We'd been hearing some banging around in the kitchen and guessed he was cooking up supper while Billy talked to him. As we opened the door, he was laying out bowls and spoons on the table. We came in and sat down to a steaming crab stew.

"Tom's stubborn as an old mule," Billy told us while we ate. "He won't take any liquor back here. I'm going to have to get transportation straight off the beach."

"You're lucky you can use my beach!" Tom said. He was agitated. "I'm not in favor of losing another dog. Your dog, if it comes to that. Or having my cabin smashed to pieces. I'll be lying low tonight with Sadie and Ruben, so don't be sending any of your rummies back here."

"You narrow-minded coot!" Billy exclaimed. "Here you could make a bundle and get away from these broken-down chicken coops, and you won't lift a finger to help yourself."

"I'm lifting my finger in the direction of peace and quiet," Tom replied. "Money's no answer to what's needed in my life."

That finished the discussion. He wouldn't hear any more of Billy's plans. He was good-natured about it. Not long after, he had Marina and me laughing at some tale from his early days. Finally Billy resigned himself and joined in with us.

It grew dark and Tom lit candles. We sat for another half hour, talking and drinking coffee while Sadie snuffled around below, looking for scraps. When she gave up on that, she lay down on Billy's feet, in hopes, I suppose, that she could keep him there forever. It was what we all would've hoped for, Tom and Marina and me, if we'd known how fast the end was coming. We didn't, though. Even with all the signs pointing in one direction, we didn't want to think that way. Fair warning, they say. But you have to be ready to see it when it comes.

The Interview

A TELEPHONE IS RINGING. OVER AND OVER. From some room back in the house.

Mr. Hart doesn't hear it. He's still in Tom Morrison's chicken coops, eating crab stew and dreading the future.

Want me to answer the phone?

The phone?

It's ringing.

Where?

I don't know. Where is it?

Mr. Hart looks around with a dazed expression.

Outside, rain is still coming down and they're still in the parlor, sitting on those rock-hard chairs. In darkness now. The wet weather has caused a strenuous new bout of growth in the window bushes out front. It really is time to cut them back, David thinks. He can hardly see his notepad.

He still brings the pad with him every day, believing he'll be taking notes, though he never does. Perhaps, he thinks, he's not suited for journalism, a profession requiring a bloodhound nose for the truth, wherever it lies hidden, and (apparently) an ability to write in places only a bat could navigate.

In the bedroom, Mr. Hart says about the telephone. *Can you get it for me?*

David races back and answers. At first, there's silence from the other end. Then:

Ruben? A woman's anxious voice.

He's here, David assures her. *I'm just answering for him. Wait a minute. I'll get him.*

The old man is already making his way to the phone. He mouths to David: *Must be the wife!* and slices a humorous finger across his throat.

David grins. He goes back to the parlor to give them some privacy. The small tables laden with photographs are there, evidence of Mr. Hart's long life with friends and family. While he waits, David wanders around examining them.

A head shot of a very pretty girl with laughing eyes and long, dark hair catches his attention.

There's an old wedding photo, a mass of bridesmaids and groomsmen fanned out around the happy couple. Ruben Hart and wife? The groom is too decked out in wedding finery to tell.

The next photo stops David in his tracks. It's of a fishing vessel tied alongside a pier. Three men stand on deck, gazing straight into the camera's eye. A fourth is in the wheelhouse, his face just visible through the glass. David bends closer and, despite the parlor gloom, reads the boat's name in faded letters on the bow.

Black Duck.
There it is!

He picks up the photo. The men staring out at him are young and earnest-looking, nothing like the wisecracking outlaw crew he'd imagined. They're wearing plain fisherman's overalls and heavy rubber boots. Two are solemn, and have taken off their caps in honor of the camera. The third wears a captain's hat cocked jauntily over his forehead. He's raising his hand in greeting, a teasing smile on his face, as if he knows the photographer.

None of them looks remotely like Ruben Hart, but then David wouldn't have expected him to be here. He was a kid at the time, fourteen years old. The only survivor of the *Black Duck* shooting was Richard Delucca, a man in his early twenties, according to the newspaper. There's no telling which of this crew he is, though David would bet a good amount that Billy Brady is the guy in the cocked hat.

He returns the photo to the table. It gives him an odd feeling to look into the young faces of men who will soon be dead. Their eyes announce confidently: *I have my whole life in front of me!* They have no idea of their approaching fate. Even if they'd appreciated the risk they were taking, and had "no one to blame but themselves," as the newspaper clipping said, David feels a deep regret for the waste of their lives. He wants to warn them: *Don't go. Watch out. It's not worth it!*

For the hundredth time, he wonders what happened out there in the fog. Were they machine-gunned without warning, as the most recent newspaper article he found seemed to report? Or did Rick Delucca, member of a crew caught with over 300 cases of liquor on board, a crew with a reputation for brazen escapes in the past, tell that story in self-defense? There's one person still alive who may know the answer.

In the back room, David can hear the old man winding up his conversation with Mrs. Hart.

You come home when you're ready. I'm fine here. . . . No. No. Don't you worry, I've got plenty. I'm still working on your clam chowder!

A hearty act. Reality shows up a moment later when Mr. Hart clumps back into the parlor, lowers himself onto a chair and gazes dismally at the floor.

He's gone, he announces. *Just heard it from my wife.*
Who?

Jeddy McKenzie. Died early this morning. He glances up. In the split second before he looks down again, David sees tears welling up in his sea-colored eyes. *I hope you won't mind me stopping early today. Don't have the stomach for any more.*

Of course not. So, your wife was looking after Jeddy?
She was. It's over. She'll be coming home now.
You won't be going there?
He wouldn't want me. Now you'd best go.
Can I do anything? Really, I'd like to help. I could run an errand. Whatever.

Come tomorrow, Mr. Hart says, wearily. *And bring a*

good pen to write with. You'll be hearing something that's never been told.

David leaves him sitting alone in the shadowy room, an old man haunted by a friendship broken seventy years ago. Does it have something to do with the *Black Duck* shootings? The photo of that boat and its doomed crew rises up before David again. On the spur of the moment, he decides to go by the town library one last time, in case he's missed anything. He mounts his bicycle and heads out.

The rain has slowed to a fine drizzle. David's tires slap methodically against the wet pavement. Something about the weather makes him think how Ruben Hart once rode these same roads on his bicycle. And there, in a flash, as if answering a call, the ghost of the young Ruben descends. David feels him, can almost see him, pedaling at his elbow. For a long minute, they ride together, side by side, the wind rushing past. Then it's over. The ghost departs. David pushes ahead alone. He picks up speed and races over the wet road toward the library. Time is running out. December 29, 1929, is about to arrive. Fog is rolling in across Coulter's Beach toward Tom Morrison's cabin, which means it's already thick out on the bay. All the signs, as they say, are pointing in one direction: Mr. Hart's story is coming to the end.

The Newport Daily Journal, January 2, 1930

COAST GUARD RECEIVED TIP-OFF TO BLACK DUCK'S ROUTE

LAY IN WAIT TIED TO CHANNEL BUOY, UNDER COVER OF DENSE FOG

NEWPORT, JAN. 2—The Coast Guard cutter that opened fire on the Black Duck early Sunday morning, killing three men and wounding one, was tipped off to the rum runners' route by a local police chief, according to the Coast Guard officer in charge, Capt. Roger Campbell.

An earlier report that the Coast Guard had stumbled by chance on the craft was incorrect, Campbell said.

"We got direct word from a local police chief that the Black Duck would be coming in to a beach along that coast. We knew they'd be steering for the bell buoy off West Island in that thick fog, so we tied up there to wait for them. Sure enough, they came along about three A.M."

Campbell refused to name the source for the tip. He insisted again that the rum runners were warned before his marksman opened fire with a machine gun.

Questions have been raised as to whether the victims were given adequate legal warning before they were shot down. The federal statute on the pursuit of smuggling craft requires that a shot be fired in warning before effective firing is started if a suspect fails to halt when ordered.

DECEMBER 29, 1929

WE WERE STILL SITTING AROUND TOM Morrison's table when, about 10:00 P.M., voices sounded outside the cabin.

Billy sprang up and went to open the door. Rick Delucca and Bernardo Rosario, his radio man, came in. Alfred Biggs was behind them. He'd brought his cousin Manny, from Portsmouth, along to lend a hand. Billy was surprised by that. He'd expected somebody else and gave the guy a look. He didn't like outsiders coming in on his jobs.

"Manny's okay," Alfred assured him. "I'll vouch for him personally. He's a hard worker, and you'd be doing him a good turn. His family's in need."

Billy nodded. "Well then, glad to help. We'll need an extra man out there, all right." He shook Manny's hand.

Sadie took one look at this army of strange boots coming through the door and scooted out from under the table. She retreated around the corner to Tom's sleeping quarters. Tom looked as if he would've liked to do the same. Never had there been such a crowd in his chicken coops, and never, I'm sure, had he ever wanted one. Still,

Billy was a favorite of his, and while he wouldn't shelter liquor, he'd agreed to let the *Black Duck*'s crew meet there before the job that night.

"C'mon over by the stove and let 'em have the table," he told Marina and me. We got up and sat down with our backs against the wall. Shortly, we were listening in on a discussion of logistics that must have taken place hundreds of times, for this was just another transport job in a long line of them, and nothing, including the fog, seemed specially out of the ordinary.

"I made radio contact with our vessel. She's a schooner out of St. Pierre by the name of *Mary Logan*," Bernardo Rosario began after they were all seated. "She's safely anchored and we have her position. Her captain's set to load from midnight on. He says it's pea soup out there. You can't see ten feet from your own nose."

Billy nodded at Rick Delucca. "We'll be steering by compass, heading for the bell buoys. Are the channel charts on board?"

Rick said they were there.

"All right. Now here's something else. Tom doesn't want liquor near his place. That means we'll need transport off the beach tonight as soon as we bring the hooch in. A big load like this can't lie out in the daylight."

"We need to get word to our truck drivers," Alfred Biggs said. "Somebody has to go up to Harveston right away and tell them to get down here."

"I figured that," Billy said. "Anybody want to volunteer?"

Nobody said anything. Everybody wanted to go out on the *Black Duck*. Finally Alfred spoke up. "Let Manny do it. Our vehicle's parked out there by the beach. He'd be a good one to go. He knows the roads around Harveston. Used to live there."

"Is that so?" Billy asked.

Manny shrugged. "Do I have to?" he asked his cousin. "I was hoping to be out on the boat tonight."

"You'll get your chance," Alfred said. "Just tonight, do what Billy wants. Take the car and round up the Harveston drivers. I'll give you the address where they're staying."

Manny saw there was no use arguing and slumped back in his chair. I didn't like his expression. He seemed like a whiner to me.

"We'll be down a man, the same as before, without Manny," Rick warned. "It'll take more time to load off the *Mary Logan*."

"I thought of that," Billy said. "We've got a man right here to take his place."

"And who might that be?" Alfred inquired. "Not old one-eye, I hope!"

Everybody laughed, which was mean of them. Tom put his lips together and took this rudeness without comment, but Billy wouldn't stand for it. For all his adventuring and interest in profit, Billy Brady was a loyal friend to those he cared about.

"Leave Tom out of this," he snapped at Alfred. "He sees further with his one eye than most people with their two."

"Well, who is it then?" Bernardo demanded.

What Billy said next blew the top of my head off.

"Who we've got is Ruben Hart, if he'll agree to it." Billy gazed at me, straight and serious. "Will you, Ruben? It'd be a favor you could do me after the one I did you."

Beside me, Marina sat up. "No, he won't! What a terrible idea. His father would never let him go."

"Well, that's just it," Billy said, giving me his wicked grin. "His father's not here to have a say. So I'm asking Ruben direct. Will you be a fifth man on the *Black Duck* tonight? We could use your muscle, and you'll have a night to remember, I guarantee it."

There wasn't any time to think about this amazing proposition, and even if there had been, I believe I'd have come to the same decision. It rose up through my blood on a reckless tide of defiance, the same wild feeling I'd been nursing all that year of wanting to get out and prove something to myself. Nothing I could do would hold it back.

"Yes, I'll go!" I answered. The crew laughed again because I sounded so breathless. To my left, Tom Morrison slowly shook his head, but he didn't say anything.

"Well, that's settled," Billy said. "Now it's time we went down to the beach and got aboard the *Duck*. She's gassed to the brim, ready to head for open sea. Manny will give you a lift home on his way to Harveston, Marina," he added to her. "Watch the evening newspapers tomorrow. You might catch the *Black Duck*'s name in print."

"Why would I want to do that?" Marina shot back. "It's

bad enough to have to worry about all of you. Now you're taking Ruben? He's too young and you know it!" She turned her back and wouldn't look at Billy, even when he went over to her.

"Come with me a moment," I heard him say in a low voice. When she still turned away, he took her hand and pulled her off around the corner to Tom's private sleeping quarters. I never knew what he said to her in those last minutes before we left. I heard his voice, quiet and confiding, rising and falling, and no sound at all from her. He must have told her something that came close to the right mark, though, because when they came out together, she was wiping her eyes and nodding.

"You know where she lives?" I heard Billy ask Manny while Marina went across the room to thank Tom for supper.

"Of course," Manny said. "It's Chief McKenzie's place. I've been there before."

An alarm should've gone off in Billy's head at that, and maybe a faint one did, because I saw him stop a moment and give Manny that same careful look he had in the beginning. Then Marina came back and we put on our coats. Two minutes later, we headed out Tom's door into the murk.

Looking back now, it seems that the ocean had never heaved with such a sickening roll or the fog been so glutinous as it was the night the *Black Duck* made its way out toward the schooner *Mary Logan*.

I was no seaman, but not a landlubber, either. I'd fished many times off a boat, and motored up and down the coast with friends since I was a kid. I knew West Island from sailing trips Jeddy and I had made out there for swimming and rock climbing on summer days. That evening, as we chugged out from shore, the island was invisible except for a threatening roar of surf.

We went by safely and came out on the open sea, though how Billy Brady and Rick Delucca managed to navigate at all was a mystery to me. They stood side by side in the pilot house, one at the wheel, the other lounging over the charts, bellowing cheerfully back and forth, their voices all but drowned out by the *Duck*'s big engines.

Once beyond the lighthouse, Billy turned on a new course which put the wind behind us, and we slid even faster through the blinding white mist. For over an hour we thudded along this way, until it began to seem we were trapped in an endless dream and would never see the shapes of the real world again.

At last, lights blazed in front of us and we came up on the sprawling form of the schooner *Mary Logan* anchored bow and stern to keep her in place. Billy and Rick had struck her right on the button. I saw them raise their fists and touch knuckles in a kind of boyish glee. And when I think of it now, they still were partly boys at heart, taking pleasure in battling dangers that would've made older men sweat.

It took us over an hour to load the liquor onto the *Duck*. The *Mary Logan*'s captain was a niggler, intent on keeping his decks clean and his hull buffered against the side of our boat. After he and Billy had matched tickets—in this case halved one-dollar bills did the trick—he stood aside and offered no help from his crew. I worked like the devil, and so did Billy and everyone, to bring the load on board. It was whiskey for the most part, several hundred cases at least. When we'd filled every crook and cranny on the *Duck*, we packed her little lifeboat with more cases, roped them in under canvas, and lowered the skiff astern to trail behind us.

"There's a night's worth of New Year's celebrating to be had off this!" Alfred Biggs called out with a grin.

"A week's worth, you mean!" Bernardo shouted back, bringing a laugh from everyone. We cast off. Billy revved the big engines and we began the bumpy trip back to Coulter's.

By this time, it was after 2:00 A.M. We were headed into the southwest wind now, facing the wallow of an ocean swell. My stomach started to go queasy. It wasn't improved by the closeness of the fog, which seemed to thicken as we drew nearer to land, or rather to where we thought land must be. Once again we were in a ghostly, immaterial world. Billy, who was steering by the ship's compass, cut our speed in case of miscalculation, and we went on blindly, keeping our ears tuned for the channel bells.

I was hanging out over the starboard rail, wondering if Tom Morrison's crab stew was about to make an early exit, when I heard Rick Delucca bellow.

"Dead ahead! What's that?"

We weren't doing more than about five miles an hour. The sound of a bell buoy rang out, and all at once I saw a black shape rising up through the murk not fifty feet in front of us.

In the pilot house, Billy swore. He goosed the engines to try to swerve. A second later, we all recognized what it was. A Coast Guard cutter, one of the big seventy-five-footers, was tied to the bell. We came up on it fast and passed close, our bow going just under theirs. We'd no sooner cleared than a light shone straight at us, a horn sounded and something whizzed past my head. From behind me came the crash of splintering wood. It took me a few moments to realize what was happening. I heard that machine gun rat-a-tat-tatting, but it didn't seem real.

By the time I caught on, bullets were slamming into the deck on all sides and the glass in the pilot house had shattered. Somebody screamed to take cover. I flung myself over the boat rail and hung just above the water. In the pilot house, a commotion had broken out. I looked and saw Billy go down. He fell over the wheel and Rick leapt to pull him up. Then the boat began to weave and lurch like a bronco. She'd veer one way, then another, and it was clear that no one had control of the wheel. I was trying to hang on and climb back over the rail, but after a violent swerve my hold broke. Off I came on a wave and dropped into the sea.

The sudden cold took my breath away. I clawed to get up the side again, but the boat suddenly bolted out of reach. Then the lifeboat was on top of me, hitting me on the head. I went for it like a drowning man, which I nearly was, and managed to haul myself into it and slide under the tarp. There I lay down on top of a pile of liquor cases.

Never have I been so cold in my life. I wasn't trembling so much as shimmying from head to foot, and I curled myself up for what little warmth I could get. Meanwhile, the lifeboat careened after the *Duck* on its twists and turns, and a fear began to build in me that we were pilotless. I remembered Billy describing how, after his dad was shot, his boat had plowed into the rocks and exploded. When I raised the tarp to look for the shore, an icy slap of seawater hit me in the face.

Finally, the ride quieted. From the waves' motion, I sensed that we were circling around. Someone was at the *Black Duck*'s helm, though I didn't yet know who. Then we must have come up on the Coast Guard cutter again. I heard Rick Delucca's voice shout out:

"Put up your guns! I've got wounded men aboard!"

A guardsman barked back, "You're under arrest. Bring your boat alongside!"

Rick did that. He'd no sooner touched hulls than two guards leapt onto the *Duck*'s deck and grabbed him. I was spying out from the lifeboat and saw how they dragged him onto the cutter, blood gushing from his hand. In short order, the *Duck* was lashed to the cutter's side, and my lifeboat was hauled in from where it had been bobbing to stern. I had a bad moment thinking those guards might be curious about what was under the tarp. They roped the lifeboat tight behind the *Duck*'s stern and never bothered to look. After that, I kept my head down and had only my ears to tell me what was happening.

Rick Delucca was putting up a fight. The guards were trying to take him down into the cutter's cabin. He kept pleading to stay on deck.

"My friends need help," he cried over and over. "They're hit. They're bleeding! Let me go back aboard."

They didn't allow him that liberty as far as I could tell. I don't think anyone else went over onto the *Duck*, either. An order was called out to cast off the bell, and the cutter got under way.

Later, the newspapers would report that "three rum-runners" all died instantly in the rain of bullets. I know that's not true. Someone was alive for a while. I heard moans and knocking sounds from the *Duck*'s afterdeck, though by the time we made Newport, all was quiet up there.

The guards tied their cutter up to a pier, unroped the *Duck* and cleated her to a separate piling. I heard them take Rick Delucca away. He wasn't saying much by then and, with all the blood he'd lost, was probably in shock. I know I was. I was shaking and quaking under the tarp so hard that it's a wonder nobody noticed and came to find me.

After a while, the cutter sped off and the *Black Duck* sat unattended. The cutter's captain went down the dock to call for medical help. He was Roger Campbell. I heard the crew address him several times. I wish now I could've risked taking a glance at the man I'd heard so much about, but I stayed low. Another half hour passed before the last of the guardsmen disappeared into the nearby Coast Guard station. I saw my opportunity and crept out.

It was dark, still too early in the morning for any show of sun. A bunch of Canada geese had flown into the harbor. They were huddled close to shore, honking in that sad, bleating way geese have when they're cold and wondering where their next meal is coming from. I went up on the *Black Duck*.

Three bodies were lying together on her deck where the guards had dragged them. I went over and looked down. They were on their backs, shoulder to shoulder— Billy Brady, Bernardo Rosario and Alfred Biggs. Their eyes were closed and at first they didn't seem that dead to me. They looked peaceful. It was as if they'd been stargazing, or telling stories to each other like boys on a camping trip, and had fallen asleep together looking up at the sky.

Except something was out of place. Someone had tried to put Billy's captain's hat back on his head. It was leaning crooked over one ear, a thing he never would've allowed in life. I reached out and took it off, but the spell was broken: I knew those men weren't ever going to wake up again.

After that, I didn't touch them. I stood back, holding Billy's hat against my chest. The wind was cold. Seawater slapped against the pier, sounding tired and bored, as if after all nothing much had happened. I felt sick. There should've been more fury going on, people screaming or the sea howling over who was lying there. I saw how murderously quiet death is, how even Billy Brady with all his charm and wit wasn't going to be able to talk back to it. That scared me worse than I'd ever been scared before. I got off his boat and ran down the pier.

Nobody saw me leave. I skirted the naval docks and took off down the road. The newspapers never got wind I was there that night. The Coast Guard didn't find out. Rick Delucca never let on, either, I don't know why. Maybe he was protecting me, or maybe he just forgot. He was in and out of court for the next two weeks, being arraigned and charged with violating the Prohibition laws. In the end, some deal went through, the charges were dropped and they let him go. People said he was never the same afterward.

I wasn't, either. I went home that day to my parents and Aunt Grace, and I stayed there. All the things I'd been doing before, I started up with again. They were good for me suddenly. The store was a good place to work. School was okay, and I did well there. I went on to the high school and when my father told me there wasn't enough money to go away to a four-year college, I didn't mind. I didn't want to go anyhow. I went over to a technical college that had started up in New Bedford and got a degree in business administration. Then I came right back and helped Dad run the store.

The laws banning liquor had been repealed by then. They went out in 1933 when the whole country voted against them. It had begun to sink in that the violence that came from keeping liquor out of people's hands was a lot worse than the violence of people drinking to their hearts' content.

I knew the truth of that more than I wanted to. For years afterward, Billy Brady walked into my line of vision every time I saw a speedboat tear down the bay, or I came across a fisherman on the beach with his dog.

I never told my parents or Aunt Grace I'd been out on the *Black Duck*. I never told any of my friends at school. The newspaper articles about the killings appeared, and I kept silent. When Roger Campbell and his crew were cleared of wrongdoing, people around here went crazy. They believed the government was covering up a crime. Still, I never gave my opinion about it. The funny thing was, even though I'd been there on the spot, I wasn't sure myself whether the Guard had given us fair warning.

There are times when truth becomes invisible, I think, beyond the reach even of those who believe they're closest to it. And so I've never talked about what happened, or tried to describe it to anyone all these years.

With the exception of one person.

MARINA

≈≈≈≈≈≈

THE MORNING AFTER THE SHOOTING, BEFORE
I went home, I stopped by the McKenzies' house.

Dawn was just breaking when I got there. I'd hitched
a ride out of Newport on a milk truck heading for one of
the big dairies on our side of the bay, then walked the rest
of the way into town. My clothes had dried, but I knew I
probably looked as bad as I felt. I stayed off the main
street, hoping no one would see me.

I didn't knock. The kitchen door was open as I knew
it would be. I hadn't been there for months, but everything looked the same. The kitchen table was in its place
under the lightbulb, already set for breakfast. The counters were neat, and Mrs. McKenzie's china was put away
carefully in its corner cupboard. I went by her portrait in
the front hall and felt her eyes follow me as I turned up
the stairs. I went slowly, on my toes, avoiding a creaky
board I knew at the top.

Nobody was up. Chief McKenzie was snoring in his
bedroom down the hall. Jeddy's door was open a crack. I
peeked in and saw him buried in his blankets.

I slipped by to Marina's bedroom, went inside and

closed the door behind me. She was sound asleep, her hair tossed across the pillow. I was afraid to wake her. I wished I could keep the news I had to tell her to myself. I wished she'd never have to hear it.

After only a minute, she knew I was in the room. Sleep is porous that way. There's usually a window raised somewhere in the unconscious mind. Her eyes opened and she looked straight at me.

"Ruben? What is it?" She sat up.

"Something's happened."

"That's Billy's hat," she said.

"Yes." I still had it in my hands.

"The *Black Duck*'s in trouble?"

I nodded. "We ran into the Coast Guard."

"Billy's in jail?"

"No."

"In the hospital?"

"No."

"Well, where is he?" she asked. Then she looked at me and knew.

It was the worst thing I'd ever had to see in my life, to watch her face cave in the way it did. I couldn't think of what else to do, so I went over and sat on her bed and put my arms around her. I started to tell her what had happened. Halfway through she began to cry. When I got to the place where we came on the Coast Guard cutter tied to the bell buoy, where the machine gun went off and the *Duck* veered away, she covered her face and told me to stop.

"I can't hear any more."

So we sat together listening to the morning sounds outside the window. A rooster's plain-and-ordinary cock-a-doodle-doo. A car's motor starting up. Someone whistling a church tune out on the road.

Footsteps sounded in the hall.

"My father's up," Marina said.

"Don't let him know I'm here."

She went across to the door and turned the lock. When she came back, she asked in a whisper:

"Was it Roger Campbell's cutter tied up to the bell buoy?"

I said it was.

"He's the man who fired on Billy's dad. Everybody knows he's loose with his guns. Billy thought he was crazy, and maybe he is. He was after the *Black Duck*, ever since they led him on that wild chase up the bay onto a sandbar."

I said I remembered that.

"If he was tied up to the bell, that means he was expecting somebody."

"It seems like it," I said. "No one would be out there otherwise. The fog was too thick. You couldn't see ten feet."

"I think he was tipped off," Marina said. "Somebody knew the *Duck* would be coming that way."

"Who?" I asked.

"I don't know." Her eyes filled with tears again. "Everyone around the bay was rooting for them. They kept clear of the syndicates and they didn't carry guns. I know Billy was on the wrong side of the law, but who would want to set a man like Roger Campbell on him?"

We looked at each other and didn't know. It would be a few days before Marina read, along with the whole town, the newspaper story about a local police chief who'd called up the Coast Guard and done just that.

The Last Interview

DAVID PETERSON IS STANDING TRANSFIXED on the front porch, a pair of brand-new hedge clippers from Peterson's Garden Shop in his hands, as Mr. Hart finishes this last bit of his story.

Chief McKenzie was the tip-off man?

That's what the caller said.

I knew it! That double-crossing rat. Was it to stop Marina from seeing Billy Brady? Or because the Black Duck *was running liquor in the New York mob's territory? Or was Roger Campbell paying him for information?*

Mr. Hart shrugs. *Any one of those reasons would do. And probably would've done if Ralph McKenzie had made that call.*

Wait a minute. He didn't?

No.

But, who did?

Mr. Hart turns to look at the progress David has been making on the bushes over the front windows. *You sure are clearing a space there. I'll be sunbathing in the parlor before long.*

Who called? David asks again.

It wasn't the chief. He wasn't at home when Manny brought Marina back from Tom Morrison's that night. Jeddy McKenzie was there, though.

David stares at the old man. *Manny Biggs ratted on the* Black Duck? *His own cousin was on board.*

He was playing for more money, I guess. He knew he'd get paid for his information, probably a lot more than Billy would've paid him for rounding up the truckers in Harveston.

So Manny told Jeddy about the Black Duck's *trip out to the* Mary Logan *that night.*

I believe so. Left a message for the chief is probably what happened.

And Jeddy called the Coast Guard?

He had to. It was police business. He was stepping into his father's shoes.

How did you find this out?

Jeddy told me.

David sits down on a porch chair. *When?*

I stopped by his room on the way out of the McKenzies' house that morning. I wanted to tell him the Black Duck *had been caught. He said he'd made the call. "How could you?" I asked him. "You don't know what you did."*

"I know what I did," Jeddy said. "I was following the law."

David looks out across the lawn, which needs cutting. Out by the road, a single dead, leafless tree limb is poking through the swirl of greenery. It should be taken down before it causes harm by falling itself, he thinks. It might drop on a car coming in the driveway, or a person walking out there.

What happened then?

What happened was the chief packed up. He and Jeddy left town. Everybody wanted to get rid of Chief McKenzie by then. The Black Duck was a hero to our folks. They all read the newspaper article and thought the chief had been the tip-off man. He covered for Jeddy, and they went down south to . . .

North Carolina, David says.

That's right.

And Jeddy never came back.

No. I never saw him again. Marina visited every few years. After the chief died, that is. She couldn't forgive her father for what she thought he'd done to Billy Brady. She never guessed the truth. I wasn't going to tell her and Jeddy certainly wasn't, either.

You must hate him, David says to Mr. Hart. You must hate Jeddy McKenzie's guts.

I don't. It was all too much for him, I think. He'd believed in his father, and in police business, and in the clear divide of right and wrong. Fog wasn't something Jeddy could deal with.

Mr. Hart takes his glasses off and wipes his eyes. *The thing is, he was a good kid. Like you. He was trying to find his way, trying his best to do what was right.*

For a long moment, they sit quietly together, gazing at the yard. Then David gets up and starts in again on the bushes with the new hedge clippers.

He can't imagine how he'll ever be able to write all this down.

AN ARRIVAL

STRANGELY, EVEN AFTER THE STORY IS OVER, and he knows everything, and nothing is left to be told, David Peterson doesn't stop going by Mr. Hart's house. He rides over the next day, and the next, and the next. There's a lot to be done around the yard. David cuts and prunes, digs and snips, plants and grooms. He takes down the dead tree limb out by the road. He's good at this work and, out of sight of his father, really enjoys it. The old man is happy to have him. They talk easily back and forth.

Have you written my story down yet? Mr. Hart asks.

No, David admits.

Well, get going. I'm not going to last forever!

I don't know how to start.

At the beginning, Mr. Hart says. *At Coulter's Beach, when we found that body. I've still got Tony Mordello's tobacco pouch, if that'll get you going.*

Is the half fifty-dollar bill still in it?

Where else?

The old man goes in his bedroom and comes out with a limp leather pouch that looks as if it's been squashed under a mattress for most of its life. Which it has, Mr. Hart acknowledges. He never found a better place.

Open it, he orders. David does, and there amid the now almost scentless crumblings of what used to be tobacco leaf, he finds the old half bill, wrinkled and pale with age, but still giving off an aura of intrigue.

You take it, Mr. Hart says. *I don't need it anymore.*

Really? The pouch, too?

It's yours. Time it passed to somebody else.

Thanks! I'll keep it safe.

I know you will.

I hitched down to Coulter's Beach the other day. Tom Morrison's shack isn't there anymore, David says.

Mr. Hart nods. He's spruced himself up this morning. His hair is slicked back. He's wearing a clean shirt. Broom in hand, he's been sweeping off the porch, all the while keeping an eager eye on the driveway. He heard from his wife last night. She's coming home today. Could arrive anytime.

Tom's chicken coops went out in the 1938 hurricane, Mr. Hart says. *Tom didn't care. He'd died and gone to the town cemetery five years before. I used to wonder how he was bearing up in such a civilized place, with all that company.*

David grins. *What happened to Sadie? After Billy was killed, I mean.*

She stayed on with Tom just as you'd expect. Became a great crabber. Marina and I went down there from time to time. Tom always cheered us up. He was one of those that carry on no matter the hardship. It showed you what was possible.

I walked around that cemetery, David says. *I found Eileen McKenzie's grave.*

Mr. Hart answers with a grunt. *That cemetery has a good part of the town in it now. At least the part I grew up with.*

I saw John Appleby's name on a stone. Is that him?

Must be. He died young. A hunting accident is what they said. I always wondered. He was the kind of stinker nobody likes having around.

Fanny DeSousa, Mildred Cumming, Charlie Pope.

Yes, they're all there. Mildred just died, lived to be ninety-six. People last a long time around here. Did you see the Hart plot in the south corner? It's where I'm headed. My father and mother are both in residence. Aunt Grace, too. She never could find anyone who knew the score better than she did.

I saw them. I couldn't find any McKenzies besides Eileen.

Nope, and you never will. Jeddy wouldn't want to come back dead any more than he did alive. I don't even know where the chief is buried.

What happened to Marina?

This question goes unanswered, and when David looks up from the bush he's attacking with the clippers, he sees Mr. Hart staring at him. His glasses give off an amused glint. *If you don't know already what happened to her, I guess I won't tell you.*

At that moment, the sound of wheels comes from the driveway and a taxi pulls up. Mr. Hart drops his broom like a hot potato. He gives his hair one last swipe, straightens his shirt and hustles down the porch steps to greet it.

She's here! he cries to David. *She's come back at last!*

AUTHOR'S NOTE

THERE ARE TIMES WHEN HISTORY SEEMS SO close, you can almost reach out and touch it.

The beaches and coastal inlets around my small Rhode Island town are unchanging places where the past can still wash in on the tide, bringing the same dark nights, sudden lights, disembodied voices and sounds of speedboat engines known to residents here during the 1920s rum-running era. My father recalls being awakened, at age eight, by a commotion on the shore below his family home. Bootleggers! Breathless, he watched from his window as their headlights danced across the sand.

Black Duck was written out of this immediate local memory, and features a notorious rumrunner craft of that name, which really did smuggle thousands of cases of liquor in to our shores during Prohibition before meeting her final fate. Manned by a crew of four from communities around Narragansett Bay, the *Black Duck* ferried goods off foreign ships from Canada, Europe and the West Indies. These boats moored along the southern New England coast outside U.S. territorial limits, beyond the legal reach of the Coast Guard. Rum Row, they came to be known, and as the decade wore on, their numbers increased until a variety of freighters, schooners, sailing craft and fishing boats stretched for miles at sea, each awaiting contact with a shore runner like the *Black Duck*.

There wasn't much the government could do about this. America's 1919 Prohibition law against the consumption or sale of liquor pitted a poorly funded assortment of policing agencies against a black market driven equally by the country's mounting thirst for liquor and the enormous profits up for grabs to those who could supply it. The *Duck* was just one among many smuggling craft, some locally owned, some built, funded and backed by crime syndicates, competing against each other along the shore, often with bloody results.

The *Black Duck*'s crew ran its smuggling operations at night, the darker the better, and often in bad weather to avoid detection. A true speedboat of her day, she was outfitted with a pair of 300-horsepower World War I airplane engines, enabling her to outrun most government boats. In addition, the men on board knew their coast well, and had the advantage of friends and allies onshore who could help them hide at short notice. Over time, their narrow escapes took on a sort of Robin Hood–like aura. And when, on the night of December 29, 1929, the crew was fired on, in dense fog, by a Coast Guard cutter that had apparently been lying in wait tied up to a bell buoy, the reaction in local communities was outrage. Three men died in a barrage of machine-gun bullets; a fourth, the boat's captain, was shot through the hand.

Protest came from all sides as many questioned whether "fair warning" had been given to the unarmed boat. A riot against the Coast Guard broke out in Boston. Threats were made against the family of the skipper who ordered the shooting. There was vandalism of Coast Guard stations, and politicians responding to public outcry demanded that the guardsmen involved be charged with murder and brought to trial. The furor carried all the way to Washington, D.C., where lawmakers, already alarmed by the dramatic rise in smuggling-related violence, began to look with new eyes at the problem. Demands were made in Congress for repeal of Prohibition. Meanwhile, reporting on the incident increased the general public's awareness of the pitfalls of enforcing such regulations. Opinions wavered, then were swayed. Four years later, in December of 1933, the "noble experiment" for enforced sobriety in America ended when Utah became the thirty-sixth state to ratify the Twenty-first Amendment, repealing the law.

Within weeks of the killings, the skipper and crew of patrol boat CG-290 were cleared by a grand jury of all wrongdoing. "Fair warning" was given the smugglers, the Coast Guard insisted. Testimony was recorded in court to back this up. And yet doubts remained, and have remained down to the present, as to what really occurred out on the water that foggy night. Did the Coast Guard, either by design or in frustration, fire without warning on an unarmed vessel? Was this a case of authorities bringing undue force to bear? Even more interesting, had CG-290 been tipped off to the *Black Duck*'s route? If so, who was responsible: a competing crime organization, or an honest citizen attempting to uphold the law? The mystery remains unsolved to this day.